Read Aloud

Bedtime Stories

Publications International, Ltd.

Contents

Contents

Puss in Boots

Adapted by Jamie Elder ▪ Illustrated by Susan Spellman

*P*uss was a clever cat who belonged to an old farmer. But one day, the old farmer died. Puss was very sad. He did not want to be all alone. He needed someone to take care of him. He needed to take care of someone.

Puss chose the farmer's youngest son.

Puss approached the young man. The young man had a very worried look on his face. He had many things on his mind. Puss remembered that the old farmer looked the same way once. The farmer was always worried before Puss had helped him. Puss knew just what to do.

"Please take me home with you," Puss said to the young man.

"I can't take you home with me," said the young man.

"Why not?" Puss asked.

"Because I have many things on my mind," said the young man.

"No need to worry," Puss said. "I am not much trouble."

"I can't help you," said the young man.

"But I can help you," Puss said.

"How can you help me?" the young man asked.

"Just give me a pair of boots. I can help," Puss said.

The young man laughed, but Puss just smiled.

"All right," said the young man. "Come home with me. It couldn't hurt to have a cat that makes me laugh."

Puss happily followed the young man home. When they reached his farm, Puss stopped smiling. He could see why the young man was worried. It was not much of a farm. Puss would have to be more clever than he thought.

"Will the boots be very much trouble?" Puss asked.

"I have an extra pair," the young man said.

"Do you think maybe you have an old sack, too?" Puss asked.

"I am sure I do," the young man said. "But why?"

Puss did not want to explain. He did not want to ruin any surprises. Instead of answering, he just smiled again. The young man shrugged and laughed. He found his extra boots. He found an old sack.

"Thank you very much," Puss said.

"You are very welcome," said the young man.

Puss waved to the young man and went toward the forest. On the way, he gathered some good grass. He put the grass in the sack. When he found a nice tree, he put the sack down. He tried on his boots, and they were very comfortable. Then he pretended to be asleep.

Soon a rabbit came by. He nosed the sack open and found the good grass. When he crawled inside to eat it, Puss jumped up. He tied the sack so the rabbit would not escape.

Smiling again, he began to walk to the kingdom's castle. It felt good to be so clever. He just hoped things would work out.

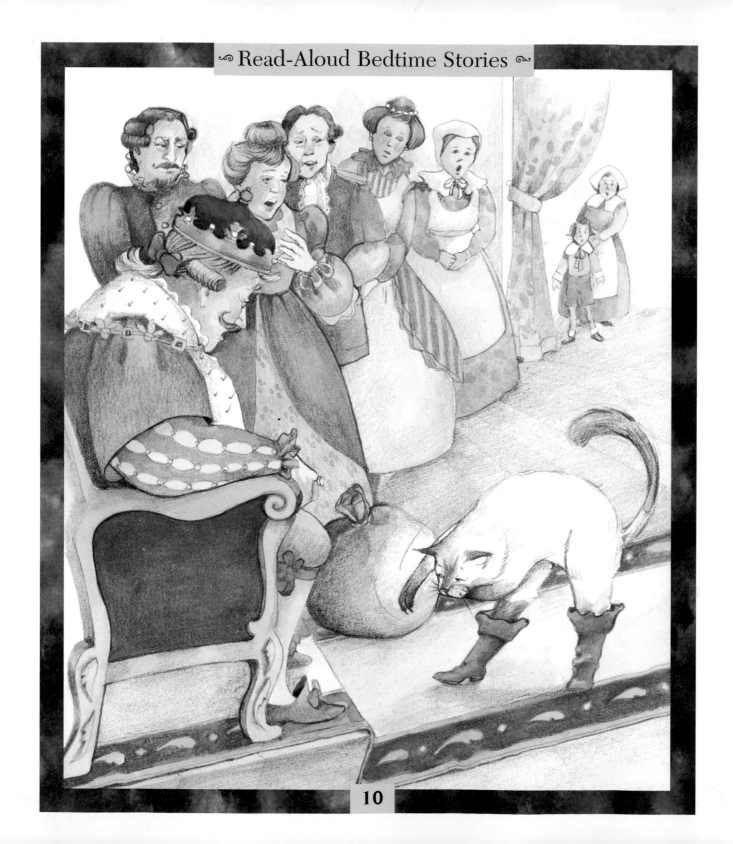

At the castle, Puss asked to see the king. He was led to the throne room. Many people were in attendance around the king. Puss almost forgot his plan.

"State your business," said the king.

"Your Majesty," Puss began, "I have brought you a gift from my master."

"Who is your master?" asked the king.

"Your Majesty, my master is the Duke of Cataclaws," Puss said.

The king was a good king, but he was forgetful. His forgetfulness was known throughout the kingdom. Puss was very clever, and his cleverness was a secret. His master was only the young man. The young man was not a duke. Puss just wanted the king to think he was a duke. Puss hoped everyone in attendance was forgetful, too.

"What is the gift?" asked the king.

"Your Majesty, it is a fine, fat rabbit. The Duke of Cataclaws wanted you to have a fine feast," Puss said.

"Thank your master for me," said the king. "I accept his gift with pleasure."

Puss bowed to the king and smiled. Everything was working out just fine.

Puss returned to the castle the next day. He brought two plump birds from the Duke of Cataclaws. The king was pleased.

The king was pleased with everything Puss brought him that week. Each time, he told Puss to thank the Duke of Cataclaws. At the end of the week, Puss was satisfied. He knew the king would not forget the Duke of Cataclaws.

Puss returned home with a plan. It was hard to wait for the right moment. Until he could do more, he tried to amuse the young man.

"Can you stand on your head?" Puss asked him.

"No," said the young man. "Can you?"

"Can I stand on your head?" Puss asked. "Sure!"

Puss perched on top of the young man's head. They laughed. Then the right moment came. The king's carriage was coming down the road!

"Go down to the river," Puss said to the young man. "When you get there, take off all your clothes and jump in."

"What are you up to? First, boots and a sack. Now this," he said.

Puss pushed the young man toward the river. He ran after the king's carriage.

"Help! Help! The Duke of Cataclaws has been thrown into the river!"

The king poked his head out of the carriage. "The Duke of Cataclaws?" he asked.

"Yes, Your Majesty! The duke was robbed and is drowning," Puss said.

"We must help him," said the king. "He has been so good to me."

The carriage raced to the river. The water was swift. The king ordered his guards to rescue the Duke of Cataclaws.

During the rescue, Puss saw the king's daughter inside the carriage. He knew then that things were working out well.

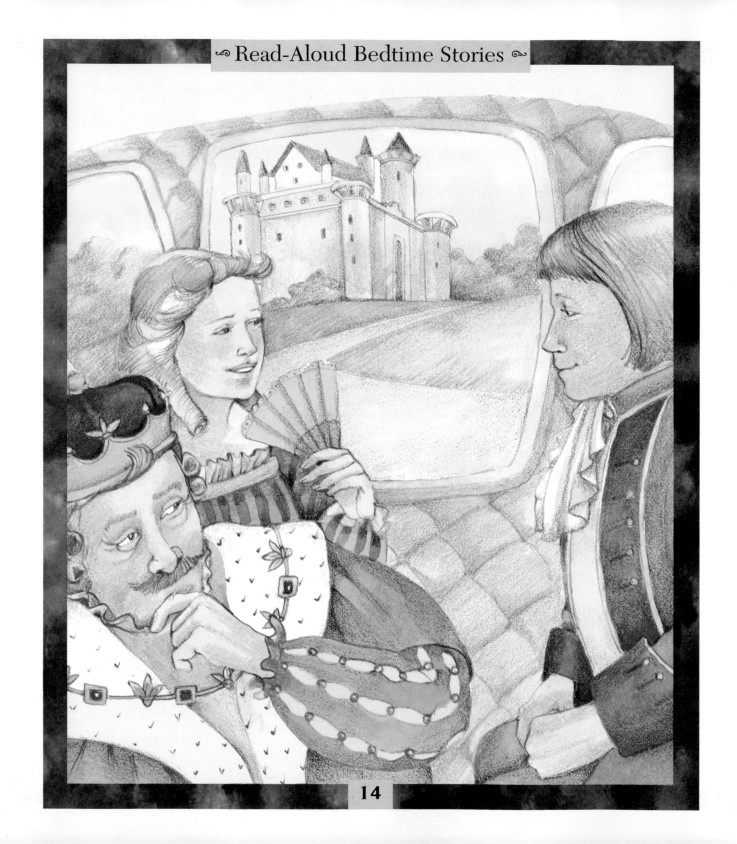

Puss went to the carriage and peeked inside. He saw the beautiful princess and smiled. She was very concerned for the young man.

"Is he all right?" she asked Puss.

"I think he will be fine," Puss said. "Of course, his clothes have been stolen. I hope he will not catch a cold."

"Nonsense," said the king. "I will have clothes brought to him."

The king sent a guard back to the castle. The guard returned with a suit of clothes. The young man put it on and looked rather fine. In fact, he looked just like a real duke.

Puss was so pleased that his plan was working.

"You must come with us," said the king.

"We are taking a tour of the kingdom," said the princess.

The young man looked at Puss. He was very confused. Puss had to think quickly to explain the young man's silence.

"The Duke is humbled by your invitation," Puss said.

"Please enjoy this time with us," said the princess.

"He is delighted to be among you," Puss said.

"Thank you," the young man finally said.

Puss jumped down from the side of the carriage. The young man stepped inside. Puss ran ahead of the carriage.

His work was really just beginning.

Puss ran fast to carry out his plan. He had to speak to everyone along the way. He came upon two farmhands first.

"You are working very hard," Puss said to the farmhands.

"These are the giant's fields. We must work hard or be cut to pieces," the first man said.

"Actually, that is why I am here," Puss said.

"You are going to cut us into pieces?" the second man asked.

"No!" Puss said. "I am only here to tell you about the giant. The king has just made him the Duke of Cataclaws."

"There is the king's carriage now," said the first man.

"Yes," said Puss. "The king will ask you who owns this land. If you say the Duke of Cataclaws, the king will be impressed. He will know the giant cares about his title. In turn, the giant will be pleased with you for being so clever. You may not have to work so hard."

"It would be nice not to have to work so hard," the second man said.

"What would happen if you told the king the wrong thing?" Puss asked.

"We would be cut to pieces," the first man said.

"Oh! Here comes the king now," Puss said.

The farmhands bowed to the king as he approached.

"Who owns this land?" asked the king as the carriage stopped.

"The Duke of Cataclaws," both men said at the same time.

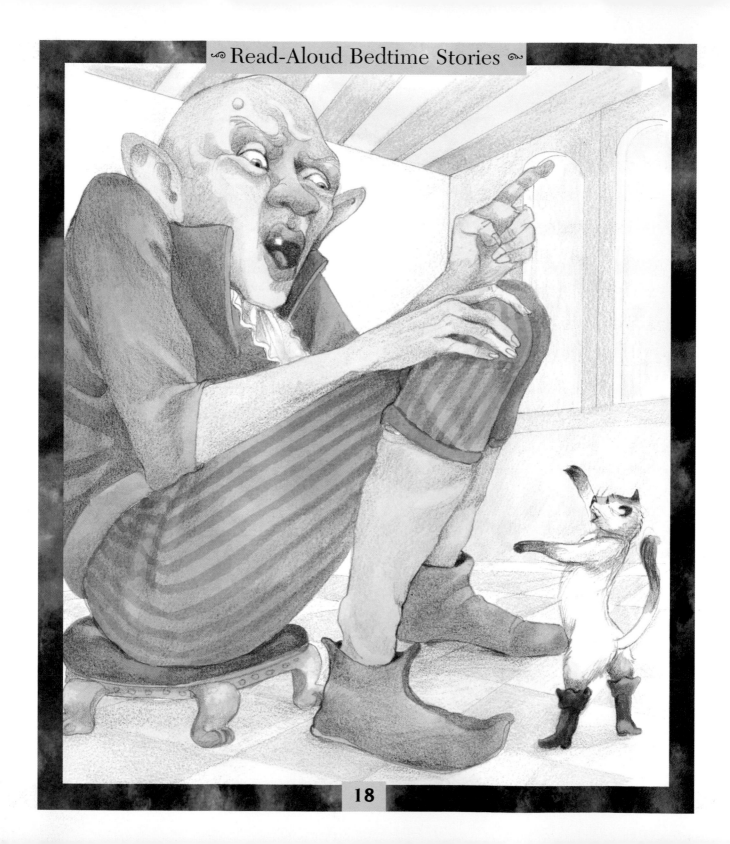

Puss could see that the king was pleased. The king really believed the young man was the duke. Puss could also see the young man and the princess. They were smiling at each other.

Puss waved to everyone and ran ahead. His biggest task was before him. He had to take care of the giant. He hoped again to be clever enough. He did not want to be cut to pieces. He just wanted to help the young man.

He arrived at the giant's castle and demanded to see him. Inside a huge hall, the giant sat on a stool. He didn't look very comfortable. Puss didn't feel bad about that.

"I hear you have special powers," Puss said.

The giant just sneered at him.

"That's what I thought," Puss said. "I didn't believe what I heard."

"What did you hear?" the giant asked.

"I heard you could turn into any sort of animal," Puss said.

"It is true," the giant said.

"But probably not a great lion, right?" Puss asked.

The giant answered him by turning into a great lion. Puss was a little bit frightened. For the giant, he pretended to be really scared.

"A lion is a great thing to turn into. You probably don't bother with small animals, though," Puss said.

"Not usually," the giant said.

"That's right," Puss said. "I didn't think so. I knew you couldn't turn into something like a mouse. That would be impossible."

The giant growled at Puss. Puss thought he was about to be cut into pieces. Instead, the giant turned into a tiny mouse.

Puss wasted no time. He pounced on the mouse. He opened his mouth and gobbled it up.

There was no more giant.

He was able to do it just in time, too. The king's carriage arrived at the castle just at that moment. Puss ran to greet it.

"Welcome to the castle of the Duke of Cataclaws!" Puss said.

"This is your fine castle?" the king asked the young man.

The young man looked at Puss. Puss smiled at him and nodded. He hoped the young man trusted him enough. He had been very clever. All he wanted was to help the young man.

The young man turned to the king. He smiled and nodded just like Puss had done.

"Won't you come inside?" the young man asked.

It was then that Puss knew everything was going to be fine. He had been clever enough. He had helped the young man. The young man was never meant to be a farmer. He was meant to be a duke.

And Puss knew he would like being a duke's cat.

❧ What a Good Man Does ❧

Adapted by Lisa Harkrader ■ Illustrated by Debbie Pinkney Davis

22

Mr. and Mrs. Goodley lived on a small farm. They had been married for forty years. They had been happy for forty years. They were happy because they always agreed.

Mr. and Mrs. Goodley had a neighbor. His name was Chauncey. Chauncey could not believe they were so happy. He wanted to know their secret.

"How do you do it?" he asked them.

"We never argue," said Mrs. Goodley. "I always agree with my husband."

"And I always agree with my wife," said Mr. Goodley.

"You can't agree about everything," said Chauncey. "You have been married for forty years. In all those years, you have never disagreed? You must have disagreed about something."

"Why would we disagree?" asked Mrs. Goodley. "My husband is a good man. What a good man does is always right."

"I agree," said Mr. Goodley. "My wife is a good woman. What a good woman does is always right."

"I agree," said Mrs. Goodley.

"Nobody agrees all the time," said Chauncey.

"We do," said Mrs. Goodley.

"That's right," said Mr. Goodley.

Chauncey knew there was something that would make them disagree.

Chauncey stayed awake all night thinking about it. Two people could not always agree! That was impossible. There had to be something. Something would make them disagree. He knew it. It was just hard to think of the right thing. Then he thought of something.

Mr. and Mrs. Goodley had two prizewinning cows.

Mr. Goodley loved those cows. He fed them. He milked them. He brushed dirt from their tails. He cleaned mud from their hooves. He even talked to them like they were people.

Chauncey knew Mr. Goodley would never part with his cows. But he decided to talk to Mrs. Goodley about them.

"Why do you need two cows?" he asked her. "You and Mr. Goodley don't drink much milk. One cow is plenty. You should sell the other one."

"You're quite right," said Mrs. Goodley.

When she called her husband inside, Chauncey was pleased. He did not think it would be so easy to convince her.

"It's time to sell a cow," she told her husband.

"Sell a cow?" said Mr. Goodley. "Our cows are prizewinners. They've never been apart. You really want me to sell one of them?"

Mrs. Goodley nodded. Mr. Goodley was quiet for a long time.

Chauncey smiled. He was certain they would finally disagree. This was about Mr. Goodley's cows, after all.

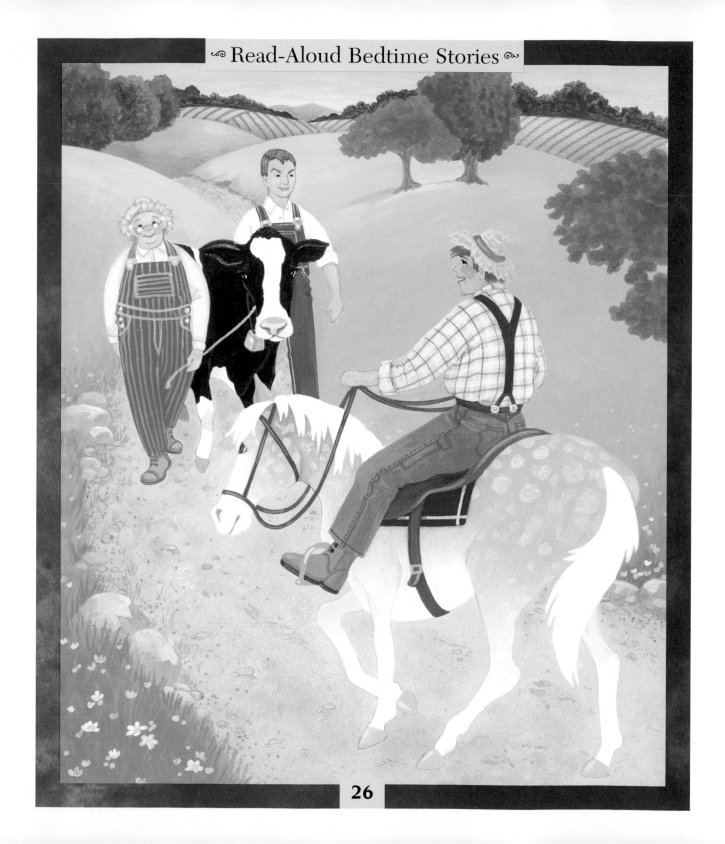

"How sensible!" said Mr. Goodley. "It's the most sensible thing I've ever heard! We don't need two cows when one will do."

"One cow is less work," said Mrs. Goodley.

"That's right," said Mr. Goodley

"One cow eats less grain," said Mrs. Goodley.

"That's also true," said Mr. Goodley.

"And the one cow will soon have a calf," said Mrs. Goodley.

"Then we will have two cows again!" said Mr. Goodley.

Chauncey could not believe it.

He watched Mr. Goodley feed both cows. He watched Mr. Goodley milk them. He watched Mr. Goodley brush the dirt from their tails. He watched Mr. Goodley clean the mud from their hooves. Mr. Goodley even talked to them.

Then he took one of the cows to town. Chauncey went with him.

Nobody in town wanted to buy Mr. Goodley's cow.

On the way home, they met a man with a horse.

"This man might want your cow," Chauncey said. "You could trade it for his horse."

Mrs. Goodley would never agree to a horse, thought Chauncey.

"That's a good idea!" said Mr. Goodley.

He traded his cow for the horse.

Chauncey smiled.

They continued walking. Chauncey stayed quiet for as long as he could.

"You started with a prize cow," he said. "Now, you have a swaybacked horse. Your wife will be surprised."

"Yes, she will," said Mr. Goodley. "We need a horse to pull our cart. I think it's sensible. My wife will think it's sensible. We always agree."

Chauncey almost believed it, but he was not ready to give up. Soon, they met a man with a pig.

"This man might want your horse," said Chauncey. "You could trade it for his pig."

Mrs. Goodley would never agree to a pig, thought Chauncey.

"That's a great idea!" said Mr. Goodley.

He traded his horse for the pig.

Chauncey smiled.

They continued walking toward home. Chauncey stayed quiet for as long as he could.

"You started with a prize cow," he said. "Now, you have a loud, squealing pig. Your wife will be surprised."

"Yes, she will," said Mr. Goodley. "We can raise piglets to sell. I think it's smart. My wife will think it's smart. We always agree."

Chauncey almost believed it, but he was not ready to give up. Soon, they met a man with a goat.

Mr. Goodley traded his pig for the goat.

He traded his goat for a sheep.

He traded his sheep for a goose.

He traded his goose for a duck.

And he traded his duck for a rooster.

Chauncey smiled.

They continued walking. Chauncey stayed quiet for as long as he could.

"You started with a prize cow," he said. "You have ended up with a skinny, scrawny rooster. Your wife will be more than surprised."

"Yes, she will," said Mr. Goodley. "The rooster will crow each morning when the sun rises. We'll never sleep too late again. I think it's brilliant. My wife will think it's brilliant. We always agree."

By that time, Mr. Goodley and Chauncey were very hungry. They passed an inn. Mr. Goodley looked at Chauncey.

"It's a shame I didn't sell that cow," said Mr. Goodley. "I would have money to buy our supper."

"The innkeeper might want the rooster," Chauncey said. "You could trade the rooster for our supper."

"Splendid idea!" said Mr. Goodley.

Chauncey could not believe his luck! Mr. Goodley would go home with nothing. Mrs. Goodley would be upset. They would disagree for sure.

Mr. Goodley traded his rooster for their supper. He and Chauncey ate until their bellies were full.

They started toward home again. Mr. Goodley did not have a cow. He did not have a horse. He did not have a pig. He did not have a goat. He did not have a sheep. He did not have a goose. He did not have a duck. He did not even have a rooster. He had nothing.

"Your wife won't like this," Chauncey said.

Chauncey felt a little bit bad for starting the whole thing.

"Oh, yes, she will," said Mr. Goodley. "I'm pleased, so she'll be pleased. We always agree."

"Not this time," said Chauncey. "I'll bet you a hundred dollars. I'll bet she will be furious."

"I'll take that bet," said Mr. Goodley. "She won't be furious, and I'll win that bet."

When they reached home, Mrs. Goodley was waiting.

"You sold the cow!" she said.

"No," said Mr. Goodley. "Nobody wanted to buy her. I traded her for a horse."

"A horse! How sensible!" said Mrs. Goodley. "We need a horse to pull our cart."

"Yes, we do," said Mr. Goodley. "But I traded the horse for a pig."

"A pig! How smart!" said Mrs. Goodley. "We can raise piglets to sell."

"We could," said Mr. Goodley. "But I traded the pig for a goat. I traded the goat for a sheep. I traded the sheep for a goose. I traded the goose for a duck. And I traded the duck for a rooster."

"A rooster! How brilliant!" said Mrs. Goodley. "It will crow every morning. We'll never sleep late again."

"That's exactly what I thought," said Mr. Goodley.

"Yes," Chauncey said. "But that isn't all. Tell her what happened. Tell her how you traded the rooster."

"Well," said Mr. Goodley. "All that trading made us hungry. I didn't have any money. I had to trade again. I gave the rooster to the innkeeper. The innkeeper gave us supper."

"You traded the rooster for your supper?" asked Mrs. Goodley. "You left with a prizewinning cow. You came home with a belly full of supper. Did I get that right?"

Mr. Goodley nodded. Mrs. Goodley was quiet for a long time.

Chauncey did not smile this time. He waited to see what Mrs. Goodley would say. He knew that Mr. and Mrs. Goodley were about to disagree. He had not meant for it to get so terrible. He had not meant to cause so much trouble. He felt bad.

It was one bet he was not going to like winning.

"How wise!" said Mrs. Goodley.

"Wise?" Chauncey asked.

He was surprised.

"Oh, yes," said Mrs. Goodley. "You both had to eat. You both needed strength to walk home. And Mr. Goodley didn't have to carry a rooster all the way. How wise and how thoughtful!"

"Thoughtful?" Chauncey asked.

He was shocked.

"Oh, yes," said Mrs. Goodley. "I won't have to cook tonight. My husband has already eaten his supper."

Chauncey shook his head. He gave up. He could not win. He handed Mr. Goodley a hundred dollars.

"You were right," he said. "You two agree on everything."

"You see how clever my husband is?" said Mrs. Goodley.

"Clever?" Chauncey asked.

"He couldn't have gotten a hundred dollars for our cow," said Mrs. Goodley. "So he traded her. He kept trading until he traded for supper. Now, he has a full belly and a hundred dollars. My husband is a good man."

"And what a good man does is always right," Chauncey said.

"Yes," said Mr. and Mrs. Goodley. "We agree."

Chauncey finally believed it.

❦ The Nightingale ❦

Adapted by Brian Conway ▪ Illustrated by Robin Moro

The emperor of China had the most beautiful palace. People came from all over the world to see it.

The rooms were huge. The windows were covered with draperies of the finest silk. The rugs were made by the best craftsmen in the world. The furniture was of the highest quality.

One hundred gardeners worked in the palace gardens. They took care of thousands of plants. They grew and tended the rarest flowers.

People came to see these beautiful things. They wanted to see things they had never seen before. They toured the palace and the gardens and were amazed at every turn. They wanted to see more when the tour was over.

"Don't let our trip end," they said.

The head gardener heard them. He knew where there was something more beautiful than any palace. It was more beautiful than any garden.

"I can show you the most beautiful thing in all of China," he said.

He led the visitors to a forest of very plain trees. He took them to one tree in particular. He pointed at a bird on a branch. The visitors looked up.

"What is so beautiful about that?" they asked. "You led us all the way out here? You wanted us to see a plain gray bird?"

"It is no ordinary bird," the gardener said. "It is a nightingale. Just wait."

The nightingale opened its mouth. He started to sing. His voice was beautiful. The nightingale made everyone feel joy.

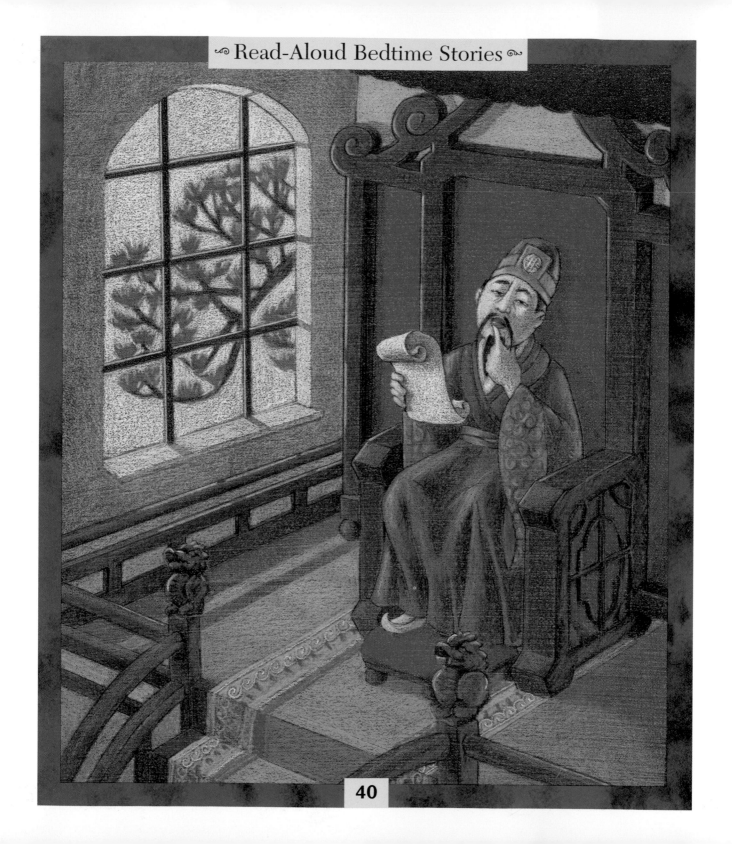

The visitors left with the memory of the nightingale's song. They told their friends about the bird.

More people came to visit the palace. But they came for a different reason now.

Everyone wanted to see the nightingale. Everyone wanted to hear his beautiful song. Everyone wanted to feel joy.

The nightingale became known as the most beautiful thing in all of China. Everyone had heard about the remarkable bird.

Everyone, that is, except for the emperor.

The emperor was very old. He stayed inside. He liked his palace. He liked the view of his gardens. But nothing brought him joy.

One day, the emperor received an important letter. It came from the emperor of Japan.

"I have heard of your wonderful nightingale," the emperor of Japan wrote. "He is the most beautiful thing in all of China. Some people say he is the most beautiful thing in all the world. I must see this wonderful bird. I will arrive in two days to pay you a visit."

The emperor was puzzled. He called for his prime minister.

"The emperor of Japan is coming to see my nightingale," he said. "He thinks I have a nightingale. I do not have a nightingale. What will I show the emperor of Japan when he arrives?"

The emperor called all of his guards together.

"Find me this beautiful nightingale," he said.

His guards tried to do as they were told. They searched from the bottom of the palace to the top. They looked under every table and over every windowsill. They searched through every inch of the palace. They could not find the bird that everyone had heard about.

"A beautiful nightingale?" they asked. "Nightingales are not beautiful. They are such plain birds. Where will we find a beautiful one?"

The guards went to see the emperor at the end of the day. They had not found a beautiful nightingale. They had not even found a plain one.

"The emperor of Japan will be here soon," the emperor said. "He expects to see this nightingale. Get the servants to help you. The bird must be found. The bird must be found by tomorrow."

The servants joined the search. They searched over the grounds. They looked in the branches of the trees. They looked on the leaves of the vines. They looked in the vegetable gardens. They looked in the flower beds. There were no nightingales on the palace grounds.

The emperor had the gardeners join the search. No one knew where to look next.

No one, that is, except the head gardener. He knew where to find the nightingale. He took everyone to the nightingale's tree.

The guards hurried back from the woods. They took the bird to the emperor's throne room.

"Well," said the emperor, "what is so special about this nightingale?"

"We do not know," they answered. "It is an ordinary bird. We found the bird in an ordinary tree."

A horn sounded just then. The emperor of Japan had arrived.

"Do not let the bird out of your sight," said the emperor.

He went to greet his visitor.

"I have come a long way," said the emperor of Japan. "I cannot wait to see the wonderful nightingale!"

The emperor took his guest to the throne room.

"This is the famous nightingale?" asked the emperor of Japan. "This is the most beautiful thing in all of China? The bird looks rather plain to me."

The emperor of Japan looked disappointed. The emperor of China was not enjoying his visitor.

There was silence in the throne room.

The nightingale opened his mouth. He sang the most beautiful song anyone had ever heard.

The emperor of Japan closed his eyes to listen. He smiled and sighed.

The emperor of China closed his eyes to listen, too. He felt something he had not felt in a long time. He felt joy.

The emperor of Japan stayed for several days. He listened to the nightingale for hours. The emperor of China listened with him. They never grew tired of the nightingale's song.

After several days, the emperor of Japan had to leave China.

"Thank you for letting me hear this magnificent bird," he said. "I must find a way to thank you."

The nightingale's song filled the palace. It always brought the old emperor great joy.

It also brought visitors from all over the world.

No one wanted to see the emperor's palace or his gardens. They cared only for the nightingale.

"The nightingale sounds so lovely," the visitors said. "It is a pity he looks so plain."

Those words upset the emperor. The nightingale's song brought him joy. He was happier than he had ever been before.

"I will not allow any unkind words about the nightingale," he said.

He ordered a golden perch for the nightingale to sit on. He ordered jewels and ribbons for the nightingale to wear.

"Now he will have a fine place to sit. He will look wonderful. But it is his beautiful song that counts," he said.

"The bird looks almost as beautiful as he sounds," the visitors said.

y

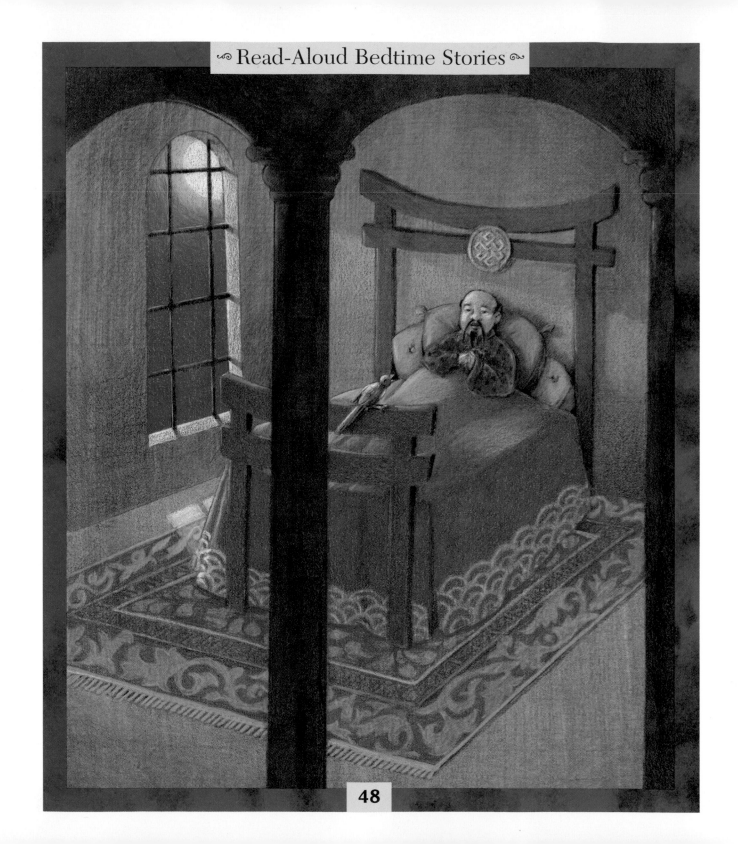

The nightingale sat on his golden perch day after day. He wore his jewels. He wore his ribbons. He sang his song. He gave many people great joy. He was nice to watch and to listen to.

But the emperor thought the nightingale looked unhappy.

"Are you tired from singing?" the emperor asked.

The nightingale continued to sing.

"You must not sing if you are tired," the emperor said. "I want you to be happy."

The nightingale continued to sing.

"You are a dear friend," the emperor said.

The emperor kept the nightingale in his private chambers at night. There were no golden perches to sit on. There were no jewels and ribbons to be worn. The nightingale could just be himself.

The nightingale perched on the emperor's bedpost. He sang his songs only for the emperor.

"You are the most beautiful thing in all of China," the emperor said. "Gold and jewels and ribbons make you look nice. They do not make you beautiful. You are most beautiful when you are yourself. You are yourself when you are singing."

The nightingale sang a special song for the emperor. The emperor felt pure joy. He drifted off to sleep.

A package arrived for the emperor. It was a present. It was from the emperor of Japan. There was a card on the package.

"I hope you enjoy this gift," it read. "It is a small token of my gratitude. You gave me a wonderful gift. The nightingale gave me great joy."

The emperor of China opened the present.

It was a small toy bird. It was brightly painted. It was covered with emeralds, sapphires, diamonds, and rubies. There was a silver key on its back.

The emperor turned the key. A song began to play. It did not sound as lovely as the real nightingale. But it would make the visitors very happy. It was very beautiful to look at.

The emperor ordered a second golden perch. He placed the toy bird upon it. He turned the key.

"Now you will have some rest," the emperor said to the nightingale.

The visitors were thrilled.

"Finally!" they said. "A nightingale that looks as lovely as it sounds!"

The toy did not sound as beautiful as the nightingale. No one seemed to care. They asked for the toy to be wound over and over again.

The nightingale no longer sang. He flew home to the forest.

No one even noticed that the nightingale was gone.

No one, that is, except for the emperor. He missed his dear friend.

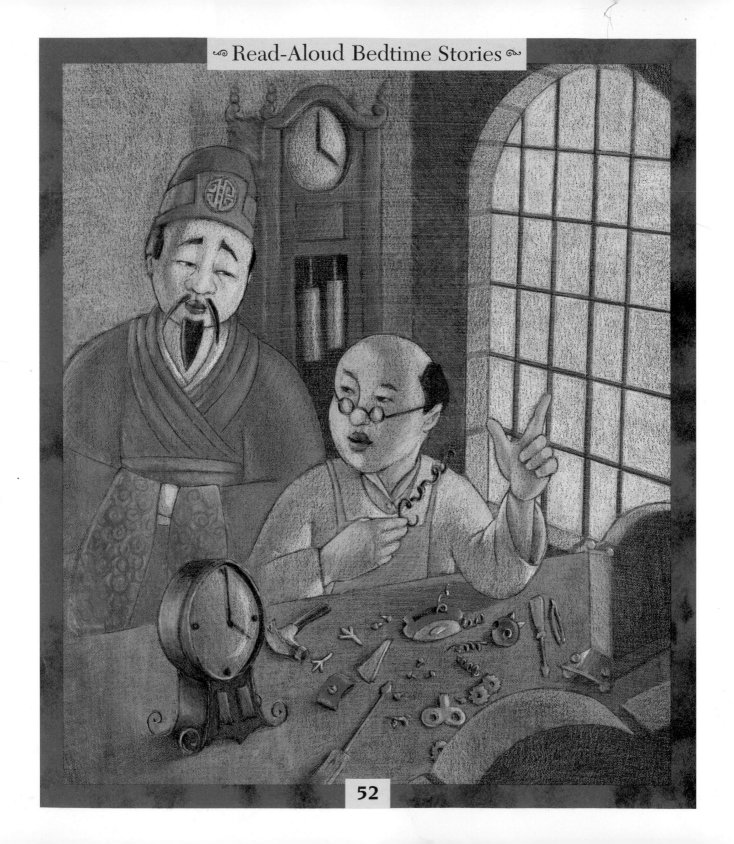

The emperor longed to hear the nightingale's beautiful song.

"I know my little friend likes the forest," he said. "It is for the best. I just hope he is happy."

The emperor's visitors were happy. They loved the toy bird's song. They especially loved the way it looked.

"Wind it again!" they said.

The emperor's servants wound the toy bird over and over again. It played all day. It played every day. It even played at night.

But something popped inside the bird one morning. There was a loud twang. The toy bird stopped playing.

The emperor shook the bird. The prime minister wiggled the key on its back. Everyone waited, but the toy bird would not play.

It was broken.

The emperor's watchmaker was summoned to the palace. He took the toy bird apart. He found out what was wrong.

"A spring has sprung," said the watchmaker. "This toy is broken."

"Can you fix it?" asked the emperor.

"Of course," said the watchmaker.

"Will it take long?" the prime minister asked. "The visitors love it."

"Not long," said the watchmaker. "But special care must be taken. It should be wound only on special occasions."

The palace became an unhappy place after that. There was no joy. No one came to visit anymore.

The emperor was sad and lonely.

He missed his friend the nightingale. He missed his beautiful song. He missed his company.

The emperor grew sick and weak. He stayed in bed.

The guards could not cheer him up. The servants could not cheer him up. The gardeners could not even cheer him up with a rare flower. No one could help the emperor.

No one, that is, except the head gardener. He knew the nightingale could help. He went to visit the nightingale.

"Your friend is ill," he said. "You should go and see him."

The nightingale flew to the emperor's window. The emperor rubbed his eyes. He smiled for the first time in a long time.

"You came back!" he said.

The nightingale opened his mouth. He sang a new song for the emperor. Tears of joy streamed down the emperor's cheeks. It was the most beautiful song he had ever heard.

He sat up in bed. The color returned to his face. He was happy to see his friend again. He knew he would hear the nightingale's sweet and special songs many more times.

The Magic Doll

Adapted by Jamie Elder ▪ Illustrated by Nan Brooks

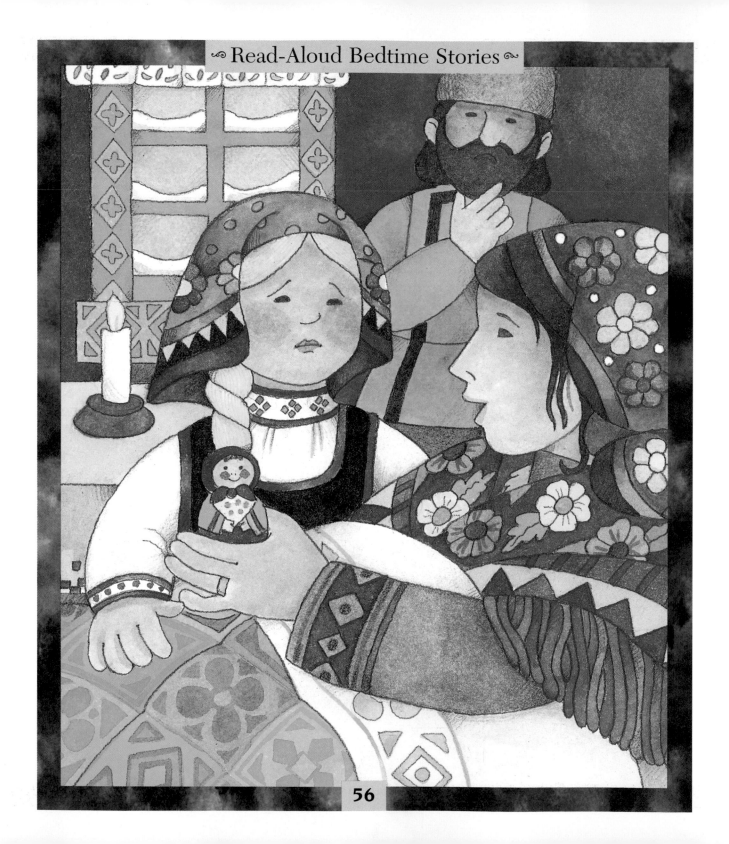

Russia is a far and distant land. Long ago, a beautiful girl lived there with her family. Her name was Vasilissa.

Vasilissa was still very young when her mother became ill. She was sick for a very long time. One night, she called to Vasilissa. Vasilissa went to her and stood by her bed.

"My beautiful daughter," said her mother, "we will not be together for much longer. I am very sick."

Vasilissa saw that her mother was holding a little doll.

"I have kept this doll for you," her mother said. "She will protect you. She will help you when you are afraid. Feed her a bit of food. Then whisper your thoughts to her. She will tell you the right thing to do. Keep her with you always. Remember that I love you. I will be watching over you."

Vasilissa took the doll. She kissed her mother.

Her mother closed her eyes. Vasilissa knew she was gone.

Vasilissa was very afraid. She took the doll out of her pocket and fed her some bread and milk. Then she whispered her thoughts into the doll's ear.

"Vasilissa," the doll said, "do not be afraid. Close your eyes and rest. Things will be better in the morning."

In the morning, Vasilissa woke up. She did not feel so afraid. She was still sad, but she knew the doll protected her. She also knew her mother was watching over her.

Vasilissa grew up to be a beautiful young woman. She took good care of her father. He was very proud of her. Vasilissa knew her father was lonely.

"Papa," she said, "you must marry again. I know you loved my mother, but you are lonely. You do not need to be lonely."

"I am not lonely when you are near," he said.

Time passed. Vasilissa's father met a woman. She had a daughter of her own. Vasilissa hoped they would all become a family.

The woman was cold and mean. She married Vasilissa's father only because he was a rich merchant. Her daughter was cold and mean, too. They were jealous of Vasilissa because she was so beautiful.

They made Vasilissa do all the hard work. They made fun of her while she did it. Sometimes, they even laughed at her.

"You aren't so pretty when you scrub the floor," said the stepmother.

"The floor looks better than you," said the daughter.

Vasilissa was afraid of them. That night, she fed her magic doll some bread and milk. Then she whispered her thoughts into the doll's ear.

"Vasilissa," she said, "do not be afraid. Close your eyes and rest. Things will be better in the morning."

In the morning, Vasilissa woke up. She did not feel so afraid. She knew hard work always paid off. She knew the doll protected her. She also knew her mother was watching over her.

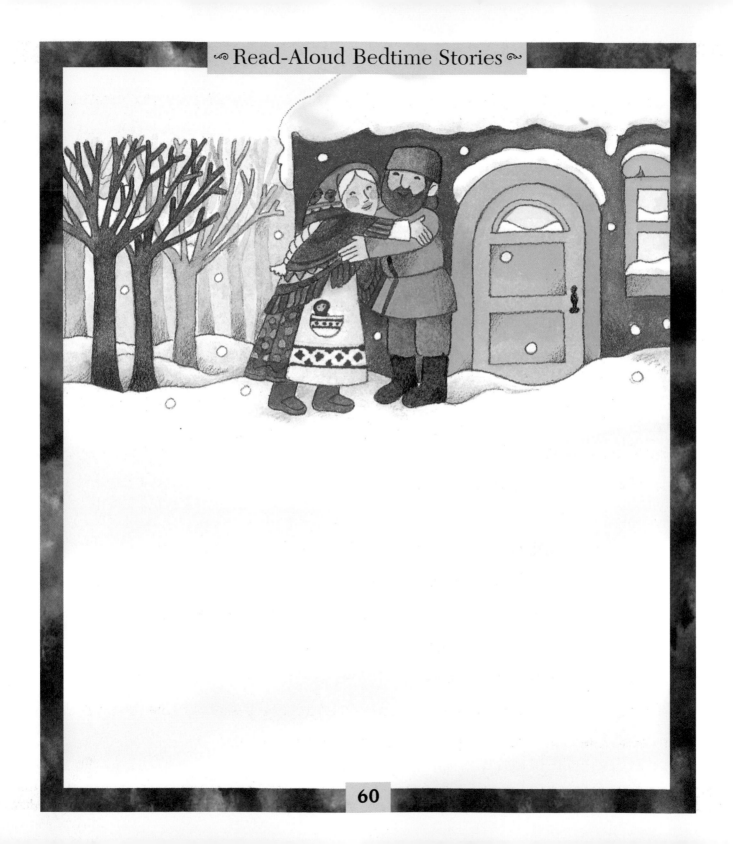

Vasilissa became more beautiful with every passing year. She was soon old enough to be married.

Young men came to call on her. The visits made the stepmother angry. She always turned the young men away.

"These men think you are beautiful," she said. "They do not know how stupid you are."

"They do not know you can't keep a floor clean," said the daughter.

"Besides, you are the youngest. You cannot marry until your stepsister is married," said the stepmother.

Vasilissa did not think anyone would want to marry the daughter. She tried not to think about it too long.

She thought about her father instead. She missed him very much. He was always away. He had to work hard. He had to make a lot of money to take care of his family.

She was afraid he would not return. That night, she fed her magic doll some bread and milk. Then she whispered her thoughts into the doll's ear.

"Vasilissa," the doll said, "do not be afraid. Close your eyes and rest. Things will be better in the morning."

In the morning, Vasilissa woke up. She did not feel so afraid. She dreamed of being reunited with her father. She knew the doll protected her. She also knew her mother was watching over her.

But Vasilissa did not know the stepmother had a plan. She sent Vasilissa to fetch water. She did not want Vasilissa in the cottage. She wanted to talk to her daughter alone.

"We must be rid of Vasilissa," she said.

"We must be careful of Stepfather," said her daughter.

"Yes," said the stepmother. "You are right. We do not want to be poor. Her disappearance must look like an accident. We will send her to Baba Yaga's house. No one ever returns from Baba Yaga's house."

It was nighttime when Vasilissa returned with the water. She found that the cottage was dark inside.

"We have no light," said the daughter.

"Go to Baba Yaga's house for a candle," said the stepmother.

Vasilissa went to look for Baba Yaga's house. It was said to be in the deep forest. It was said that no one ever returned from it.

Vasilissa tried not to think about that. She walked for a long time. She saw a light in the trees. She knew it was Baba Yaga's house when she got closer. It had to be! It stood on the bones of chickens. It was surrounded by the heads of animals. An old woman peeked out of the window.

"What do you want?" she asked.

"Only a candle," Vasilissa said.

"There is a price to pay even for a candle," Baba Yaga said.

Baba Yaga opened the door to her house. Vasilissa stepped inside. She was surprised by all the strange things she saw.

Baba Yaga had many pets. She had cats and birds. She even had snakes. She also had strange things in jars on her shelves. On the floor, there were bones and skulls.

"It is not time for a candle," Baba Yaga said. "It is time for sleeping."

She shut her eyes. She fell asleep in her strange chair.

Vasilissa did not know what to do. She disliked her stepmother and the daughter, but she wanted to go home. She did not want to end up like the bones on the floor.

She was very afraid.

She held her magic doll close to her. She did not have any bread or milk to feed her. She dared not take any from Baba Yaga. She just did not know what to do.

She stood still for a long time. She tried to remember what her magic doll always told her.

Her doll always told her not to be afraid. Her doll told her to close her eyes and rest. Her doll told her things would be better in the morning.

Vasilissa lay down on the floor. She closed her eyes. She hoped things would be better in the morning. She would just have to wait and see. All she could do was rest.

Baba Yaga woke Vasilissa in the morning. She gave her a list of chores.

"A candle is expensive," she said. "Finish everything before I return."

Vasilissa nodded. She looked down at the list. Baba Yaga was gone when Vasilissa looked up. She knew she had to work fast.

She also had to work hard. She was used to hard work. Soon, she was finished. Soon, Baba Yaga returned.

"Did you finish everything on the list?" she asked.

"Yes," Vasilissa said.

"I do not believe you," she said. "It is not possible."

"I finished everything. I promise," Vasilissa said.

"How did you do it?" she asked.

"I am blessed," Vasilissa said. "My mother is watching over me."

Baba Yaga jumped from her chair. She threw a candle at Vasilissa.

"One who is blessed cannot be here," she said. "Go with your candle!"

Vasilissa ran from Baba Yaga's house. She ran and ran until she reached the cottage. She opened the door, but it was dark inside. The stepmother and her daughter were gone. But her father was there!

"My beautiful daughter," he said. "I have missed you."

Things were always better in the morning. Hard work did pay off. She was finally reunited with her father. The magic doll did protect her.

Her mother was watching over her, too.

The Boy Who Cried Wolf

Adapted by Jennifer Boudart ■ Illustrated by Jon Goodell

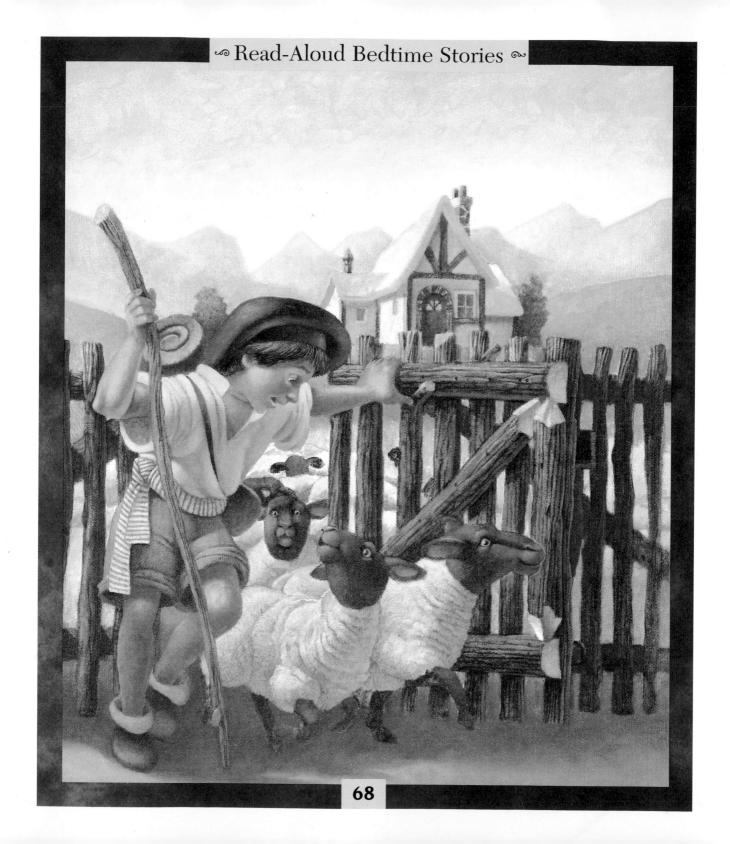

*T*he village of Woolington was known for sheep. Everybody had at least one. The doctor, the butcher, the blacksmith, and the mayor all had sheep.

What was so great about Woolington sheep? Their wool, of course! The town held a wool sale every spring. Buyers came from near and far. They came from everywhere. They brought empty carts and full pockets. They left with full carts and empty pockets.

"Woolington wool is so soft!" said some.

"It makes such warm blankets and sweaters," said others.

There was no question about it. Woolington loved its sheep. No one in Woolington loved them more than Timothy. He was the shepherd boy.

"I love the sheep," Timothy always said.

Timothy took his job very seriously. Each day, he gathered the town's sheep. He walked them down the street. He herded them to the meadow.

Timothy found the sheep the greenest grass and the coolest water. He pulled rocks from their hooves. He combed their wool.

Woolington was very proud of Timothy.

"Timothy is a terrific shepherd," said the doctor.

"Timothy treats those sheep like family," said the butcher.

"Timothy always keeps the sheep safe," said the blacksmith.

"Timothy will not let us down," said the mayor.

Timothy's father had taught him everything about herding sheep.

"A shepherd boy must keep his sheep safe," Timothy's father said. "That is the first rule."

Timothy never forgot that rule. While he was on the job, he did not take a nap. He did not read a book. He only watched for trouble.

Maybe he did daydream a little. But he never had any real trouble. A lamb might try to run away. A dog might scare the sheep. A sheep might get its foot stuck in a hole. Those were small things.

"Watch out for wolves," Timothy's father said.

But Timothy had never seen a wolf in the meadow. He had never seen a wolf anywhere.

"Wolves must live way up in the mountains," he thought.

Timothy could see Woolington from the meadow. He watched people open their shops. He watched them hang out their wash. He watched them eat lunch. He watched other children play.

Timothy was bored sometimes. Every day was exactly the same. Get the sheep. Walk with the sheep. Watch the sheep. Take the sheep home. Timothy wanted to play like the other children.

Timothy tried to play with the sheep. He found out they were not very playful. They just chewed the grass when he kicked a ball. They just twitched their tails when he told a joke. The sheep did not want to play.

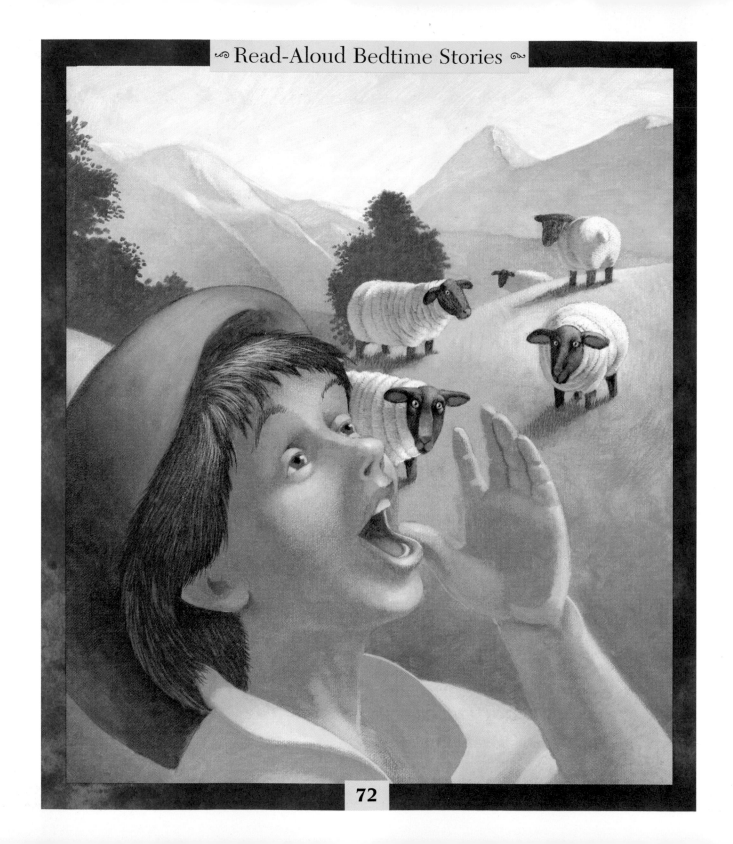

Timothy was sitting in the meadow one morning. He looked up at the sky. He gave each cloud a name for its shape. Flower cloud. Butterfly cloud. Wagon wheel cloud. Wolf cloud.

The last cloud gave him an idea. What would he do if a wolf came along? He had only his shepherd's crook. He was not very big. The wolf would not be scared of him. Timothy would be scared of the wolf.

What would he do? He could call for help. The people of Woolington would hear him. He had a very loud voice. Everyone would run down the street. They would rush into the meadow. The wolf would run away.

There would be three cheers for the shepherd boy. For him!

Timothy stood up. What if he pretended to see a wolf? Would the people of Woolington come running? That would be fun and exciting. Fun and excitement were just what he needed.

"Help! Help!" Timothy yelled. "A wolf is after the sheep!"

It was not true. All the sheep were there. They were eating grass. They didn't even notice when he ran behind a tree.

Timothy watched people run from their shops. They dropped their wash. They left their lunches behind. Even the children stopped playing.

"Timothy needs help!" the people said.

Everyone ran to the meadow. The Woolington sheep were in trouble. Their shepherd boy was in trouble!

Never had there been so many people in the meadow. They all rushed up the hill. Their shouts filled the air.

All the sheep were there. The people of Woolington were confused.

"What is this?" asked the doctor.

"I do not see a wolf!" said the butcher.

"The only thing out of place is Timothy," said the blacksmith.

"Maybe the wolf dragged him away!" said the mayor.

That got everyone shouting and running again. They looked for wolf tracks. They looked for any clues about what had happened. One boy spotted Timothy's crook. It was next to a big tree. He ran to pick it up.

"Timothy is here," he said

Everyone looked at the big tree. Timothy came out from behind it. He took a few steps and fell down. He was shaking all over.

"Are you all right, Timothy?" the boy asked.

"I can't stop laughing!" Timothy said. "All that running and shouting! You all looked like a bunch of sheep! You looked like you were scared silly!"

"We were scared silly," said the mayor. "Now we are angry. Making up stories about wolves is not funny. Do not play tricks like that again."

Timothy tried to say he was sorry. His giggles got in the way. He could not stop laughing.

Everyone went back to town.

When Timothy got home, there was big trouble. His father was angry.

"I didn't want to upset anyone," Timothy said. "But it was a good test. I wanted to know what would happen if there was a wolf."

Timothy also thought it had been very funny. But he did not say that.

Timothy collected the sheep the next day. People were still angry.

"I worry about these sheep every day," he said to himself. "It was nice to have people worrying about me for a change."

He was angry that nobody worried about him. He was so angry he made a decision. He led the sheep to the meadow. Then he started yelling.

"Help!" he yelled. "A real wolf has come! He is after the sheep!"

Timothy found another place to hide. The town came running. They knew right away they had been tricked.

"Come out, Timothy," said the mayor.

Timothy had never seen the mayor so angry. He went to stand in front of him. He was not laughing anymore.

"You let us down," said the mayor. "We told you not to play tricks. You did not listen. Maybe we won't believe you if you call for help again."

Timothy felt bad. The mayor was right. He had been doing more than playing tricks. He had been telling lies.

"No more lies," Timothy said.

Only the sheep heard him. Everyone else had gone back to town.

A few days passed. Timothy took extra good care of the sheep. He wanted to prove he was still a good shepherd. He sat and watched for trouble. He also daydreamed a little.

Timothy heard a strange noise during one of his daydreams. It came from one of the sheep. It was not a happy sound. It was a frightened sound.

A wolf was in the meadow! A huge wolf! It was chasing the Woolington sheep. The wolf was biting the sheep. Timothy could see its sharp teeth.

"Help! Help!" Timothy yelled. "A wolf is in the meadow! It's chasing the sheep!"

Timothy watched for someone to come running. No one did. He called for help again.

"A real wolf has come!" he yelled. "I am not making it up! I need help!"

Timothy was shouting as loud as he could. He was jumping up and down. He was waving his arms. No one even turned to look at him. Woolington might as well have been miles away.

Timothy could hear the wolf growling. He shook his crook at the wolf.

"Go away!" he said.

The wolf was not afraid, but Timothy was.

"Someone please help me!" he yelled.

There was no answer. Timothy was very afraid.

He ran all the way to Woolington.

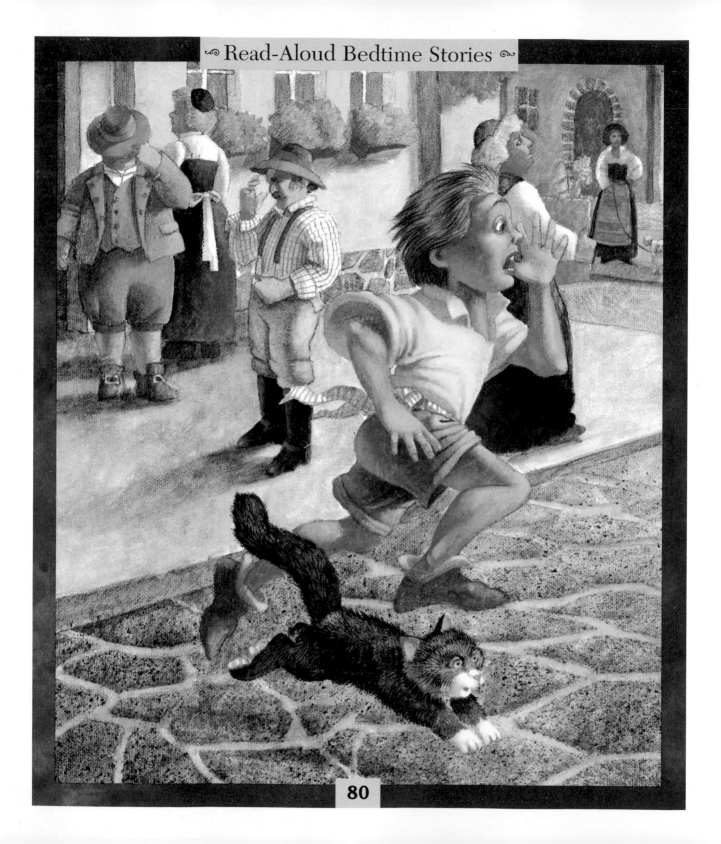

He ran from one person to the next person.

"A wolf is in the meadow!" he said.

"Stop your tricks, Timothy," they all said.

Timothy ran to the doctor.

"A wolf is in the meadow!" he shouted.

"I am not a fool," said the doctor.

Timothy ran to the butcher shop.

"A wolf is in the meadow!" he shouted.

"Very funny, Timothy. Go back to the sheep," said the butcher.

Timothy ran to the blacksmith shop.

"A wolf is in the meadow!" he shouted.

"I don't want to hear another word," said the blacksmith.

Timothy even tried to talk to the mayor. The mayor just walked away.

"I am telling the truth!" he yelled.

No one paid attention. No one believed him. He started to cry.

Timothy remembered what the mayor had said.

"Maybe we won't believe you if you call for help again," he had said.

If only Timothy had not played tricks!

He ran back to the meadow. The wolf was gone. The Woolington sheep were gone, too. The wolf had taken them all away. Timothy had broken the first rule. He had not kept the sheep safe.

Nothing was the same after the day the wolf came. It became known as Wolf Day.

After Wolf Day, Woolington was no longer famous for sheep. No one kept sheep after that.

After Wolf Day, Timothy was no longer known as the shepherd boy. He was known as the boy who cried wolf. He was also known as the street sweeper. That was the only job he could get.

Timothy was very sorry about what had happened. It did not change things though. He could not bring the sheep back.

Timothy took many walks to the meadow. He sat against a tree. He did not take a nap. He did not read a book. He did not even daydream. He thought about what had happened, instead.

He took out his pocket knife. He used it to cut into the tree trunk. He carved a message there. You can still see it today if you visit Woolington.

This is what it says:

The boy who cried wolf lost the sheep of this town.

His tricks and his lies let Woolington down.

He joked about wolves, then a real one came by.

"It's a wolf," cried the boy. They said, "It's a lie."

The boy lost the sheep. He learned something, too.

If you want to be trusted, you must always be true.

The Seal's Skin

Adapted by Brian Conway ▪ Illustrated by Linda Dockey Graves

*L*ike his father before him, Sean was a fisherman. He spent his days at work on the sea.

For Sean, the sea was a familiar place. He knew where to find fine schools of fish. He knew how to toss his net into the waves. He knew when to pull it out. He knew his net would be full of flapping fish. He was a good fisherman.

The work was easy for Sean. It was in his blood. He was born to be a fisherman. His life was simple.

But he was lonely.

The fishing boats returned to the docks each night. The fishermen shored their boats. They sorted through the fish. They folded up the nets. They hurried up to the village. They met their waiting families.

Sean's partner, Ian, had a family.

"My wife will be happy with today's catch," Ian said. "Why don't you come for supper?"

Ian invited Sean for supper every night. Sean always declined.

"Thank you, but no," Sean said. "I think I will take a walk instead."

Sean walked in the moonlight along the rocky shore. He looked up to see the village. Smoke rose from the cottage chimneys. Families were inside.

Sean did not have a wife. He did not have a family. His cottage looked dark, cold, and empty. He was not happy.

Sean walked along the shoreline alone every night.

He stared out at the sea. He loved the water. It was always in motion. It never stopped moving.

Life on land was too slow and solid for Sean. He liked to row in his boat on the waves. He would fish through the night if he could.

"The sea is a place of magic and mystery," his father used to say.

Sean had heard the legends many times. He had heard stories about mermaids, magical serpents, and sea sprites. They lived in an undersea world. They rarely showed themselves to the people of the land.

"The sea holds many secrets," his father used to say.

Sean's father always used to tell him about the seals. His father said that some seals were regular people under their skins. They could remove their smooth skins like clothes. Sometimes, they would walk on land. Sometimes, they would visit the village.

Sean's father used to point out the seals on the shore.

"Look at how big and round their eyes are," he used to say. "They look like ours. Listen to them carry on. They shout and laugh and cry and sing to each other. They are just like us!"

These were the stories that all fishermen told their children. But Sean did not have any children.

He did not believe in legends, either.

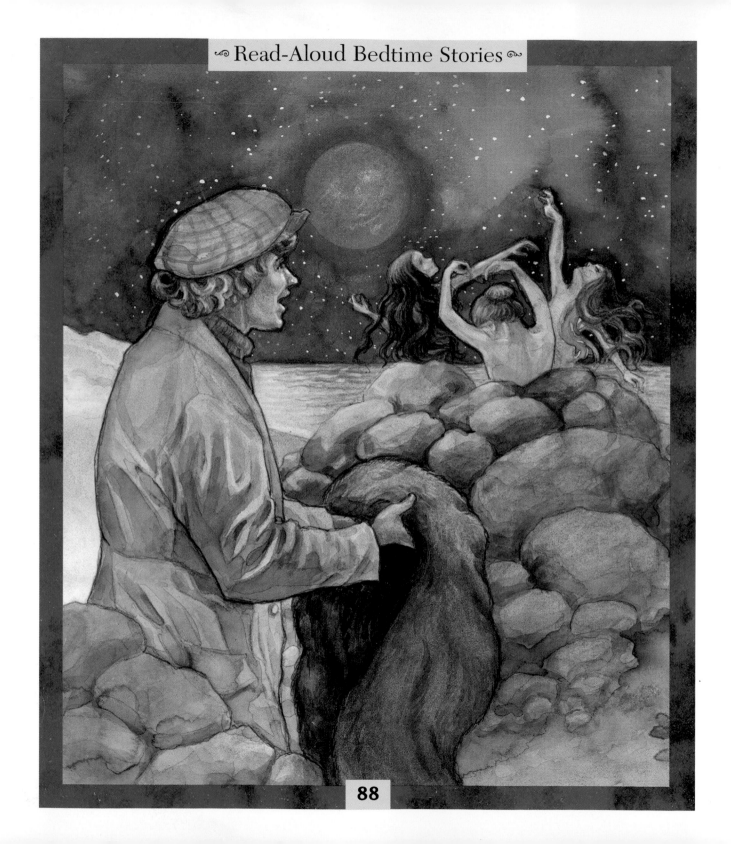

As he walked that night, he heard noises. He heard high voices and cheerful laughter. He wondered who would be out on such a cold night.

He walked quietly toward the sounds. He peeked slowly over the rocks. He saw three young women.

They danced on a flat rock beside the waves. They sang with clear voices. They were the most beautiful women he had ever seen.

He went over the slippery rocks toward them. He stepped on something. It was soft and loose. He was sure it was the smooth skin of a seal. He was very surprised.

He called out to the women.

They stopped dancing. They ran across the rock. Two of them slipped into their skins. They slid off the rock and into the tide.

The third woman ran toward Sean. She saw her soft coat in his hands. She gazed at him with a smile.

"You must choose," she said. "You can return my skin or dress me in clothes. If you return my skin, you will never see me again. If you give me clothes, I will be your wife."

Sean stared back into the woman's large blue eyes. They held the magic and mystery of the sea.

For the first time, Sean believed in the legends. For the first time, Sean did not feel lonely. For the first time, he was really happy.

Sean held the seal's skin close to him. He wanted to know things about the beautiful woman.

"You are a seal?" he asked.

"I am a seal when I am in the skin," she said. "When I am out of it, I am a person. I am like you."

"Have you ever lived on land?" he asked.

"No," she said. "I have made visits to your wonderful land. I always return to the sea."

Sean put his coat around the woman. He did not want her to get cold.

"I will give you a wonderful life here on land," Sean said. "You will have a house in the village. You will have children. You will have everything you need. You will have everything you want."

Sean looked into her eyes. He felt love.

"But you must promise to stay forever," Sean said. "You must never return to your life in the sea."

The woman looked back at the sea.

"I promise," she said. "Take the skin, and lock it away. I will wear a dress instead. I will walk on the land. I will live the life of a villager."

Sean bent down on one knee.

"Will you marry me?" he asked.

"Yes," said the beautiful woman. "I will."

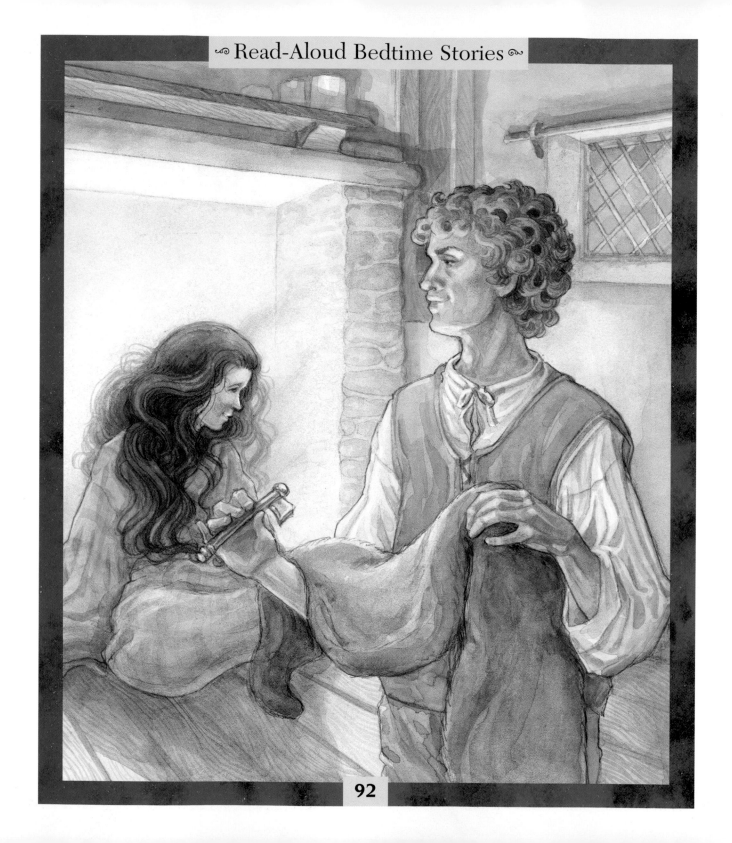

Sean took her to his lonely cottage. He built a fire. She warmed herself, and he hid the seal skin in a chest. Then he hid the key to the chest.

The woman wanted to know many things. She asked Sean many questions. She wanted to know more about life in the village.

"People love their families," Sean said. "Children are important. Work is important. Dancing and singing are important."

"It is the same with the people of the sea," the woman said. "We love our families. We work. We also dance and sing."

She smiled at the thought.

"I have always wanted to live among the villagers," she said. "Land is still a mystery to me. My new life with you will be an adventure."

"You will need a name," said Sean.

"I have a name," she said. "It is Mara."

The next morning, Sean and Mara went to the dock.

"Ian," Sean said, "I would like you to meet someone. This is Mara. She is to be my wife."

"Congratulations!" Ian said. "Where did you two meet? I have not seen you in the village before."

"We met while walking along the shore," she said. "I am from a village near here."

Ian was very happy for his friend. Sean deserved to be happy.

Mara loved her life on land. She loved Sean. She loved being his wife. She also loved all the people of the village. She learned their names. She learned their customs.

She learned the stories they told when they gathered together.

"It is strange," she said. "The villagers tell stories about the people of the sea. My people tell stories about the people of the land."

Soon, Sean and Mara started a family. They had a daughter. They named her Sela. She had large, round eyes like her mother. She was beautiful like her mother. She also loved the sea.

Several years passed. Mara and Sela went down to the dock every morning. They waved to Sean as he rowed out to sea.

Mara watched Sean row through the waves. She looked past him. She looked out over the ocean.

She missed her people. She missed the sea.

At the end of every day, Sean rushed home. The cottage was always bright and warm. His family was always waiting for him.

He always brought a fine fish for their dinner. He also always brought a pretty seashell for Sela.

But one day, it was different. He came home, and the house was dark and cold. Mara was weeping.

"I love you, Sean," she said. "I love Sela, too."

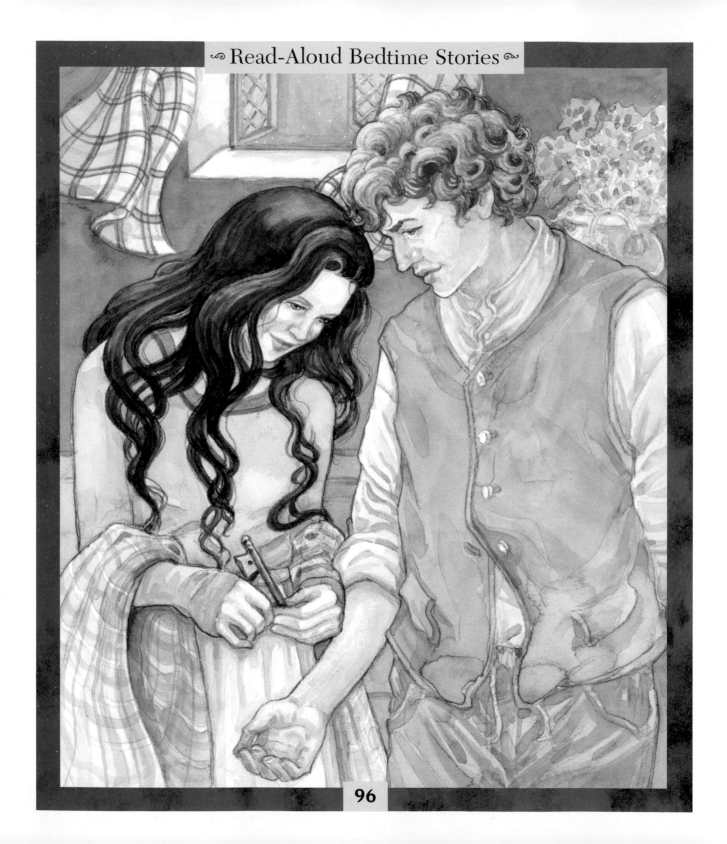

Mara's face had never looked so sad.

"Why are you crying? Why are you sad?" Sean asked.

"I love you both," Mara said. "You have made my life here wonderful. But I miss my people. I miss the people of the sea."

"We are your family now," said Sean. "You promised to stay here."

Mara looked past her husband. She stared out the window. She looked out to the sea.

"I am sorry, my husband," she said. "I did not think I would feel this way. I was not meant to live on land. I need to swim in the deep, cool waters. I need to move with the tides. I need to go back to my people."

Sean had always known this day would come. He understood Mara's longing for the sea.

"I love the sea, too," he said. "I love it more than I love the land."

"I wish I could take you and Sela there," Mara said. "You would love it."

"I wish you could, too," said Sean. "But we could not survive in the water. We do not have seal skins."

Mara hugged her husband.

"And so, you see why I cannot survive on land," she said. "The sea is my real home. You are my family, but I do not belong here."

Sean pulled an old, rusty key from his pocket. He held it for a moment. Then he put it into Mara's hand.

"This key unlocks a chest in the shed," Sean said. "There you will find your seal skin."

Mara held the key. She kissed Sean. Then she ran out to the shed.

The seal skin was neatly folded inside the chest. It was still soft and smooth. Mara clutched the skin close to her. She hurried back to the cottage.

Her face was bright and happy. Sean had seen her this happy once before. It was the first time he had seen her. It was when she had danced on the rock. She was not a seal then.

Sean and Sela walked with Mara. They walked in the moonlight over the rocky shore.

Two seals came up from the water to greet them. They called to Mara. She called back.

She turned to Sean and Sela.

"I will miss you both," she said. "I will love you forever."

The two seals slid off the slippery rock. Mara slipped into her seal skin and swam after them.

Sean and Sela walked along the shore every night. Sean told his daughter many stories about the sea. Many of the stories were legends. One story was true.

Sometimes, when they walked, a seal would appear on the rocks. They could tell it was Mara by her eyes. Sean was always happy to see her.

The North Wind

Adapted by Lisa Harkrader ▪ Illustrated by Beth Foster Wiggins

Nate's mother handed him a leather money pouch. The pouch had only a few coins in it.

"Go to the village," she said. "Buy some oats for our dinner tonight."

Nate ran to the village because he was very hungry. He bought a basket of oats.

On the way home, the North Wind began to blow. He blew into Nate's basket. He blew the oats across the field. He blew and he blew. He blew until the oats were gone.

Nate stared at the empty basket.

"I can't go home without oats for our dinner," he said.

He returned to the village and bought more oats.

On the way home, the North Wind began to blow. He blew into Nate's basket. He blew the oats across the field. He blew and he blew. He blew until the oats were gone.

Once more, Nate returned to the village. Once more, he bought a basket of oats.

Once more, the North Wind began to blow. He blew into Nate's basket. He blew the oats across the field. He blew and he blew. He blew until the oats were gone.

Nate stared at his empty basket. He stared into his empty money pouch.

Nate went to bed hungry that night. He knew his mother was hungry, too. He could not fall asleep.

He climbed from his bed. He put on his boots and mittens. He put on his heavy winter coat. He tiptoed past his mother's bed. He tiptoed out of the cottage.

"I must find the North Wind," he said. "Maybe he will give back our oats. I hope he will give them back."

Nate walked through the night. He walked through the dark and the cold. Snow swirled around him. Leaves crunched under his feet.

He was scared. He had never been so far from home before. He hoped he was going the right way. He hoped he was doing the right thing.

He kept walking. He walked through the darkest part of the forest. He walked until he came to a house made of stones. It had to belong to the North Wind.

Nate knocked at the door. It squeaked open.

A wrinkled face peeked out. It was the North Wind! Nate knew him at once. He looked old. He looked tired. But he did not look scary. Nate thought he would be scary, but he was not. He looked very kind.

The North Wind stared at Nate.

"What is it?" he asked.

His voice whistled through the forest.

"Three times I bought oats," said Nate. "Three times you blew them away. I came to get my oats back."

"I don't have your oats," said the North Wind. "It is my job to blow the wind. Once I blow oats away, they are gone. They are scattered across the fields. But you were brave to come here. I'll give you this, instead."

The North Wind handed Nate a tablecloth.

"Tell it, 'Cloth! Cloth! Serve food!' You will never be hungry again," the North Wind said.

Nate thanked the North Wind and set out for home. He stopped at an inn for dinner.

He sat down in the dining room of the inn. He spread the cloth on the dinner table.

"Cloth! Cloth! Serve food!" he said.

A roast beef sprang from the cloth. Up popped potatoes, carrots, bread, and cake. Nate ate and ate.

The innkeeper stood in the doorway. He watched and smiled. He gave Nate the very best room.

"Sleep well," he said.

The next morning, Nate ran all the way home. He ran into the cottage. He spread the cloth on the table.

"Mother, look!" he said. "Cloth! Cloth! Serve food!"

Nate watched. His mother watched. The cloth did not do anything.

Nate ran his hands over the tablecloth. He smoothed out the wrinkles.

"Cloth! Cloth! Serve food!" he said.

The cloth still did not do anything.

"I don't understand," Nate said. "It worked at the inn. The innkeeper saw it. He could tell you."

"I think you have been tricked," his mother said.

"I think you are right," he said.

Nate pulled on his boots and mittens. He put on his heavy winter coat. He set out to find the North Wind.

He walked through the day. He walked through the cold. Bushes rustled. Trees moaned.

He was scared. He knew wild animals lived in the woods. He knew they were big animals. He knew they were hungry animals. But he and his mother were hungry, too.

He kept walking. He walked through the darkest part of the forest. He walked until he came to the house made of stones.

Nate knocked at the door. It squeaked open.

The North Wind peeked out. He was surprised to see Nate.

"What is it now?" he asked.

His voice howled through the forest.

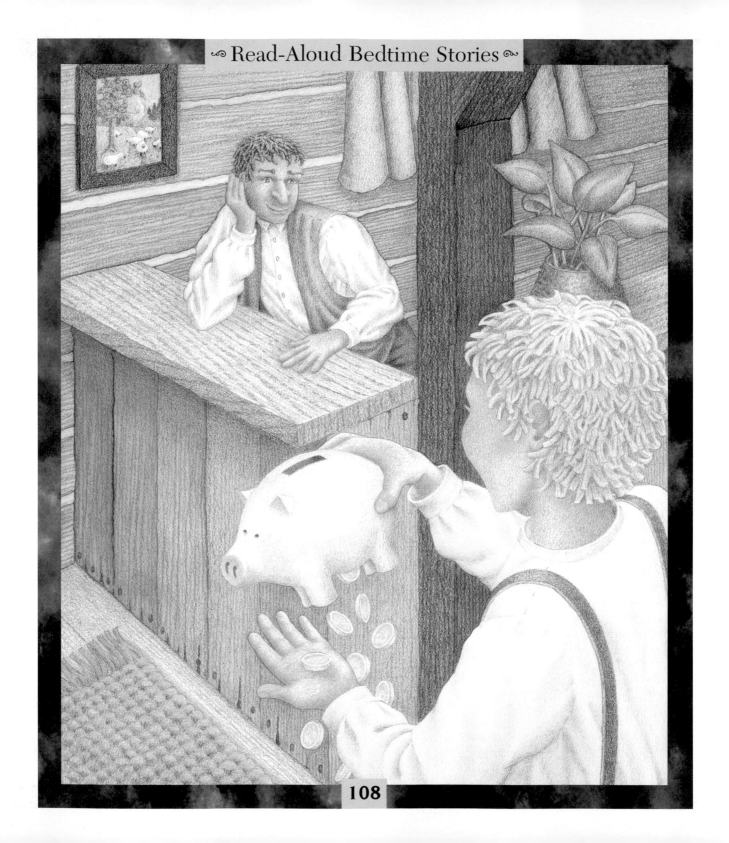

Nate handed the tablecloth to the North Wind.

"It doesn't work," he said. "You tricked me."

"Why would I trick you?" he asked. "I blow the wind. I do not have time for tricks."

"The cloth doesn't work," Nate said.

"This isn't the cloth I gave you," said the North Wind. "This one is torn and stained. But you were brave to come here. I'll give you this, instead."

The North Wind handed Nate a piggy bank.

"Say to it, 'Bank! Bank! Make money!' You will never be poor again," the North Wind said.

Nate thanked the North Wind and set out for home. He stopped at the same inn for the night.

Nate held the bank in front of him.

"Bank! Bank! Make money," he said.

Coins dropped from the bank.

Nate handed the coins to the innkeeper.

The innkeeper watched and smiled. He gave Nate the very best room.

"Sleep well," he said.

The next morning, Nate ran all the way home. He ran into the cottage. He held out the bank.

"Mother, look!" he said. "Bank! Bank! Make money."

Nate watched. His mother watched. The piggy bank did not do anything.

Nate rubbed his hands over the piggy bank.

"Bank! Bank! Make money!" he said again.

The bank still did not do anything.

"I don't understand," said Nate. "It worked in the inn. The innkeeper saw it. He could tell you."

"I think you have been tricked," his mother said.

"I think you are right," he said.

Again, Nate pulled on his boots and mittens. He put on his heavy winter coat. He set out to find the North Wind.

He walked through the day. He walked through the cold. Owls hooted. Wolves howled.

He was scared. He was afraid of what the North Wind would think. He knew the North Wind would be angry at him. But he was more afraid he and his mother would go hungry.

He kept walking. He walked through the darkest part of the forest. He walked until he came to the house made of stones.

He knocked at the door. The door squeaked open.

The North Wind peeked out. He was startled to see Nate.

"You again!" he said. "What is it this time?"

His voice thundered through the forest.

Nate handed the piggy bank to the North Wind.

"It doesn't work," he said. "You tricked me again."

"I didn't trick you," he said. "I blow the wind. I don't have time for tricks."

"The bank doesn't work," Nate said.

"This isn't the bank I gave you," the North Wind said. "This bank is chipped and cracked. Someone is tricking you, but it is not me."

"The innkeeper!" Nate said. "He tricked me. He waited until I was asleep. Then he stole the bank. He must have taken the tablecloth, too. He was always watching me."

"You were brave to come here," the North Wind said. "I have something that you can use against tricksters."

He handed Nate a rope.

"Tell it, 'Rope! Rope! Tie him up!' You'll never be tricked again," he said.

"Thank you," Nate said. "You have been very kind to me."

He set off for the inn with the magic rope.

When the innkeeper saw Nate, he smiled.

"What have you brought tonight?" he asked.

"Only this magic rope," said Nate.

The innkeeper smiled again. He gave Nate the very best room.

"Sleep well," he said.

Nate set the rope on a chair. He crawled into bed. He waited.

Nate's door squeaked open in the middle of the night. The innkeeper slipped into the room. He reached for the rope.

Nate sprang from his bed.

"Rope! Rope! Tie him up!" he said.

The rope slithered around the innkeeper's legs. It wrapped around his arms. It tied him up. The innkeeper could not move.

"Let me go!" the innkeeper said.

"After you give the tablecloth and the bank back," Nate said.

The innkeeper told Nate where the tablecloth and the bank were. Then Nate untied the innkeeper.

Nate gathered all his things and ran all the way home. He ran into the cottage. He spread the tablecloth on the table. He put the piggy bank on the cloth.

"Mother! I got the North Wind's gifts back! Look!" he said. "Cloth! Cloth! Serve food! Bank! Bank! Make money!"

A pot of stew sprang up from the cloth. Coins spilled from the bank.

"Oh, my!" his mother said. "We will always have enough to eat. We will always have enough money."

Nate nodded.

"We also have the magic rope if anybody tries to trick us," he said.

He thought of the North Wind and smiled.

Smart Manka

Adapted by Jamie Elder ▪ Illustrated by Pat Hoggan

anka loved her father very much. When he was upset, she helped him. She was a very smart young woman. He counted on her.

Her father was upset about a cow. The cow was supposed to be payment for his hard work. He had built a good fence for the farmer. The farmer did not pay him. Her father was upset. He did not know what to do. Manka was also upset, but she knew what to do.

"Father, we must go to the judge," she said. "The judge is a very fair man. He will be able to help us."

"How will he be able to help us?" her father asked.

"He will hear your story. He will know what to do," she said.

"I hope you are right," her father said.

They went to see the judge. Manka's father told the judge about the fence. He told the judge about the cow. When he was finished, the judge was quiet for a moment.

"We must ask the farmer to come," the judge said.

"Will you have him bring the cow?" asked Manka's father.

"No," the judge said.

Manka could see her father was upset again. She patted his arm.

"It is important to appear fair," she said. "You must trust the judge."

She smiled at the judge. He smiled back at her and nodded his head.

It was not long before the farmer arrived. When he saw Manka's father, he frowned. Manka looked at the judge.

"We must settle the matter of the cow," the judge said.

"There is no matter," the farmer said.

"This man says there is," the judge said and pointed to Manka's father.

"There is no matter," the farmer said again.

"Then you will know the answer to my riddle," the judge said.

"You will solve the matter with a riddle?" the farmer asked.

"You agree there is a matter then?" the judge asked.

"What is your riddle?" the farmer asked.

"Whoever answers correctly will take the cow," the judge said.

"What is your riddle?" the farmer asked again.

"Which side of the cow is the darkest?" the judge asked.

He looked at Manka. He could not smile. She could tell that he wanted to smile. She smiled and whispered the answer into her father's ear.

"What is your answer?" the judge asked the farmer.

"It is a silly question," the farmer said. "There is no answer."

"There is an answer. What is it?" the judge asked Manka's father.

"Is it the inside?" he asked.

"Yes," the judge said. "The inside of the cow is the darkest. The cow is yours," the judge said.

After the matter of the cow, Manka and the judge began to spend a lot of time together. She liked him because he was fair. He liked her because she was smart. They were a good match.

"Manka," the judge said, "I would like you to be my wife."

"I would like you to be my husband," Manka said.

"Will you marry me?" he asked.

"If you will marry me," she said.

"There is just one thing," he said. "You are very smart."

"Is that a bad thing?" she asked.

"It is a good thing. But Manka, you cannot interfere with any of my cases. People know you are smart. They will talk to you. They will think you can change my mind about my decisions. You must promise not to interfere," he said.

"I promise not to interfere," she said.

"If you should, I will ask you to leave my house. You cannot interfere with my work. It would not be right. People would talk," he said.

"I promise not to interfere," she said again. "You are also smart and will always do the right thing. I will have no reason to interfere."

"I will make you proud by making good decisions," the judge said.

"I am already proud of you," she said.

They were married that very spring. Manka moved to the judge's house.

Manka loved the judge very much. When she was happy, he was happy. When he was happy, she was happy. She was a good wife. She did not interfere with his work. He made good decisions that made her proud.

But one day, all that changed. Manka was in her garden tending the vegetables. A man she did not know stopped to greet her.

"Good day, Madame," he said. "Is your husband home?"

"No, he isn't. I would be glad to give him your message," she said.

"I have no message," he said. "I just hoped he had changed his mind about my colt."

"What is the matter with your colt?" she asked.

"There is nothing the matter with it. It just doesn't belong to me anymore," he said.

"How did that happen?" she asked.

"My mare gave birth to a colt under a wagon. The owner of the wagon said the colt belonged to him. The judge agreed with him," he said.

"That doesn't sound right," she said.

"I didn't think so either," the man said. "I couldn't argue with the judge, though. He is usually fair. I just hoped he had changed his mind by now. I need that colt."

"I think I can help you," she said.

"I would be very grateful, Madame," the man said.

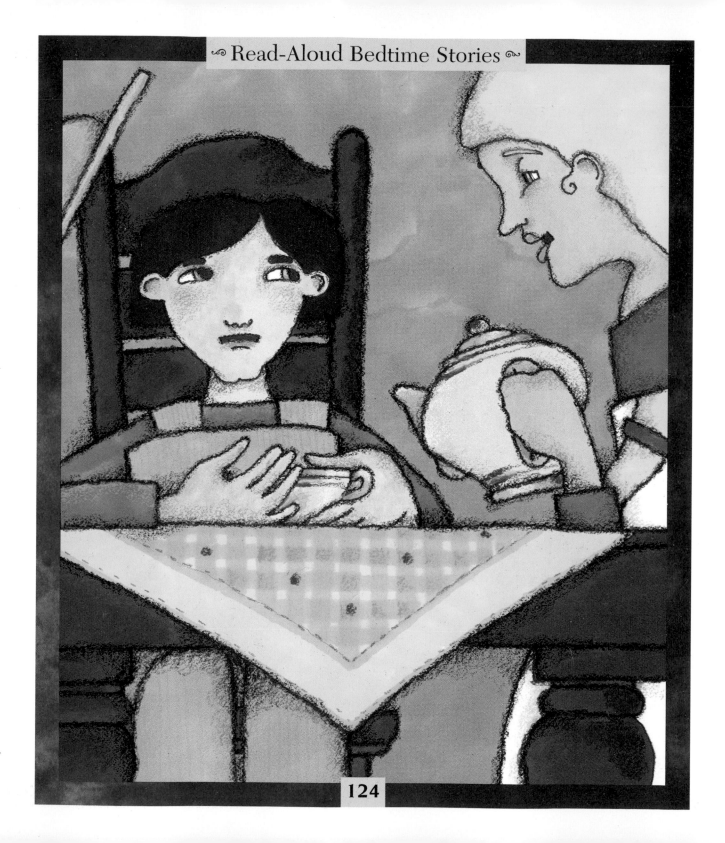

Manka invited the man in for tea. She knew she was breaking a promise to her husband. She had promised not to interfere with his cases. But this case was different. Her husband had made a very bad decision. The bad decision hurt an innocent man. She had to do something.

"Come here at lunchtime tomorrow," Manka said to the man. "Bring a fishing pole. Pretend that you are fishing in front of the house."

"That will make me look like a fool," the man said.

Manka nodded and smiled at him.

"Do not worry. It will only be for a minute," she said.

"It will make me look crazy," the man said.

"Do not worry," she said. "The judge will be having his lunch. When he sees you, he will come outside. He will want to know what you are doing."

"What will I be doing?" the man asked.

"Fishing!" she said.

"That is impossible," the man said.

"That is the point," she said. "The judge will ask what you are doing. Tell him you are fishing. He will explain that there are no fish in the road. He will want to know if you are crazy. Tell him that you might be crazy. If wagons can have colts, roads can have fish."

"That is so smart!" said the man. "I will do it."

"I am glad," she said. "Just don't tell the judge it was I who helped."

The man came at lunchtime the next day. He cast his fishing rod into the dusty road. When the judge saw him, he was puzzled. He got up from his meal and went outside.

"Sir," the judge said. "May I ask what you are doing?"

"Of course," the man said.

The judge waited a minute for the man to reply. The man just smiled and reeled in his line.

"May I ask what you are doing?" the judge asked again.

"You may ask," the man said.

"Sir, please tell me what you are doing," the judge said.

"I am fishing," the man said.

"You cannot get fish from a dusty road," the judge said.

"It is possible," the man said.

"It is not possible," the judge said. "Are you crazy?"

"I might be crazy," the man said, "but it is possible."

"How is it possible?" the judge asked.

"If a wagon can have a colt, a dirt road can have fish," the man said.

The judge was quiet. The man reeled in his line and waited. It was hard to pretend about the fish. He hoped the judge's wife was right.

"I see your point," the judge said. "Your colt will be returned to you."

"Thank you very much," the man said.

When the man was gone, the judge went back into the house. He sat across from his wife. He stared at her for a long time. He was not very happy. He was very upset.

"What is the matter?" Manka asked.

"I know it was you," he said. "You interfered. You helped that man."

"You are right," she said.

"Why did you do it?" he asked.

"I did it because you made a bad decision. An innocent man was hurt by that decision. I interfered because it was important to help him," she said.

"Oh, Manka! Think of how people will talk," he said.

"It is better they talk of me. It would be worse if they talked about your bad decision," she said.

"You are very smart," he said. "I agree with you, and I thank you. But Manka, we had an agreement. You will need to leave this house."

"I understand. We had an agreement. I broke my promise, and it is only fair. I am very sorry. I did not mean to make you unhappy. I was trying to be a good wife to you," she said.

"You have always been a good wife to me, Manka. You were a good wife even today. Please take the one thing you like most from this house. It will be my present to you. Maybe it will remind you of me," he said.

"Thank you," Manka said.

Manka and the judge ate dinner together one last time. She served all his favorite foods. He toasted her health many times with good wine. He drank so much wine that he became very sleepy.

When he was asleep, Manka loaded him into the horse cart. She put a pillow under his head. She covered him with a blanket. She drove the cart to her father's house. Her father helped her carry the judge to a bed. Manka watched him all night. In the morning, he woke up.

"Where am I?" he asked.

"I have brought you to my father's house," she said.

"Why would you do that?" he asked.

"You said that I should take one thing from the house. You said it should be the thing I liked the most. I took what I liked the most," she said.

"That does not explain what I am doing here," he said.

"I like you the most," she said.

The judge became quiet. He looked at Manka for a long time. He smiled. He laughed out loud.

"You have outwitted me again," he said to her.

"No," she said. "I am just helping you."

"Will you come back home with me?" he asked.

"Of course," she said.

"You are very smart," he said. "I need all the help I can get."

The Bell of Justice

Adapted by Brian Conway ■ Illustrated by Jon Goodell

*I*n a special little town, there hung a big bronze bell. The townspeople put the big bell in the town square.

They called it the Bell of Justice.

It was not an ordinary bell.

It was not rung on holidays. It was not rung on the mayor's birthday. It was not rung to celebrate anything.

The bell had a special purpose. It was rung only when someone needed help. Anyone who was treated unfairly rang the bell.

When it rang, the townspeople came to the square. They came to help right the wrong.

The bell served the townspeople well for many years. They were very proud of their bell. They kept the bronze brightly polished. It shone like gold over the busy town square.

The bell was for everybody. Rich or poor, old or young, and tall or short could ring the bell.

When the mayor heard the bell, he put on his robe. He called for his assistant. They went to the square to hear the problem.

All the people in town gathered in the square. They looked to the mayor to set things right.

It took only one pull of the long rope. The Bell of Justice rang. Any person could state his or her problem.

The bell was there for anybody who needed it. That was the most important thing about the bell.

The bell was not used very often. The townspeople were usually fair to one another.

The bell always shone brightly in the square. But the rope used to ring the bell was old. It was worn. It was falling apart.

After many years, the rope was nearly gone. Only the tallest person in town could reach it.

The mayor noticed the rope one day. It was terribly frayed. He went to talk to his assistant.

"This will never do," he said. "The rope on the bell is too short. Only a tall person can ring the bell now."

"Short people need justice, too," the assistant said.

"We need a new rope right away," the mayor said.

The bell was very high. They needed a long rope. They searched through the town. No one could find a rope that was long enough.

The mayor sent his stable boy to the next town. He sent him on a horse. The sooner he returned with a new rope, the better.

The mayor's assistant found a temporary solution. He tied a long grapevine to the bell. It hung down to the ground.

"Very good," the mayor said. "There will be justice for all."

An old knight lived on a farm on the edge of town.

He heard the stable boy ride past his house. He watched him as he disappeared down the road.

It made him remember his days of travel and battle. Those days were good days, but they were over. He had settled on the farm to rest. He had retired from knighthood.

He had once used the woods around the farm for hunting. He had owned many fine hunting dogs. He had owned many fine horses. His horses were the most beautiful in the land.

But the old knight did not hunt anymore. He sold all of his hunting dogs. He sold all of his horses except for his favorite.

His favorite horse had served him well. The horse had carried him through many battles. The horse had carried him through many lands. He kept the horse. He used him in festivals and in holiday parades. But he no longer really cared about the horse.

The old knight cared only about his money. He had a lot of it. He spent his days and nights counting it.

He did not like to spend it.

He stopped taking care of his farm. He stopped taking care of his horse.

The horse was no longer his favorite thing. Money was his favorite thing. He liked it more than anything else.

The knight's farm crumbled.

The stable toppled over. His old horse had nowhere to sleep. He stayed outside in the dry, rocky pasture.

The horse did not get any attention. His coat became dirty and rough. His shoes rusted, and his hooves cracked.

The knight did not buy any feed for the horse. He just gave the horse a handful of hay every day. The old horse's belly ached. He needed more than just hay.

But the old knight ran out of hay. He did not buy any more. He decided to let the horse go instead.

He opened the pasture gate.

"You're a smart old boy," he said. "Go find your own food."

It was a hot summer day. The horse wandered through the countryside. All the grass was dried up. All the streams had dried up, too. The horse had no food or water.

The horse did not understand what was happening. He knew only that he was hungry and thirsty. There was no food or water in sight. He did not know what to do.

He wandered from farm to farm. Every field had a fence around it. He saw fresh grass but could not reach it.

He had to keep looking.

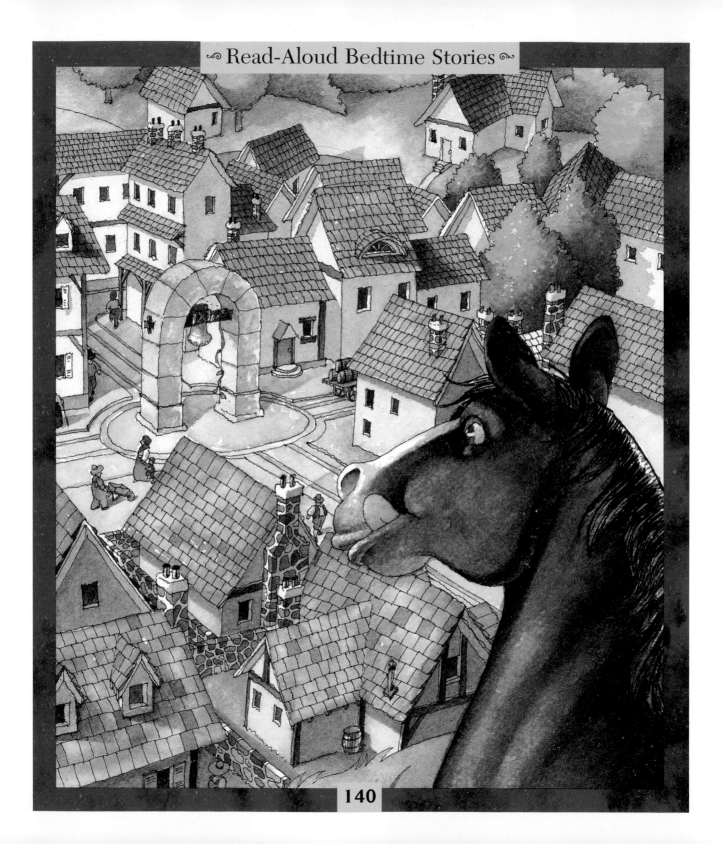

The old horse did his best to find food. He nibbled at small patches of grass along the road. He drank from muddy puddles of rainwater.

He did fine for a while. Whatever he found was more than the knight had ever given him. It was still not enough to do him much good.

He started to get sick.

The old horse became thinner and thinner. His legs grew weak and frail. His head hung low. He was too tired to hold it up.

He became very sick.

But he kept walking.

He followed the road to a town. He saw people bustling about. He heard happy people laughing and talking. He smelled food.

Then the hungry horse spotted something wonderful. He could hardly believe his eyes.

He opened his eyes really wide. He stretched his neck forward to see. His mouth began to water.

He saw a long green vine. It was hanging in the center of town. It was tied to a shiny bell. Some of its thick green leaves were low to the ground.

The leaves were bright in the sunlight. The leaves were even brighter than the shiny bell.

The horse ran as fast as his legs could carry him. He ran down the hill. He ran toward the town square.

The horse ran up the main road into town. He passed many busy people. No one seemed to notice him.

His eye was on the long vine. There was a huge leaf on it. It was the lowest one. It looked especially delicious.

He stood under the bell. He sniffed the vine. It smelled very good. He could hardly wait to taste it.

He closed his eyes. He took the leaf in his mouth. He snipped it off the vine with his teeth.

He chewed the thick green leaf. It was so fresh and juicy. It was delicious. He could not remember the last time he had eaten. He could not remember when he had eaten anything so wonderful.

He worked his way up the vine. He snipped off the next leaf with his teeth. He chewed and swallowed. He started to feel a little better. But he was still very hungry.

He began to eat faster. He took the lowest leaves on the vine one by one. Each one tasted better than the one before.

There were more leaves on the vine. The old horse could not reach them. But he was still very hungry. He pulled on the vine to reach more.

He pulled hard. The bell sounded with every pull. The horse kept reaching for the leaves. He rang the bell over and over again.

The good people of the town went to the square.

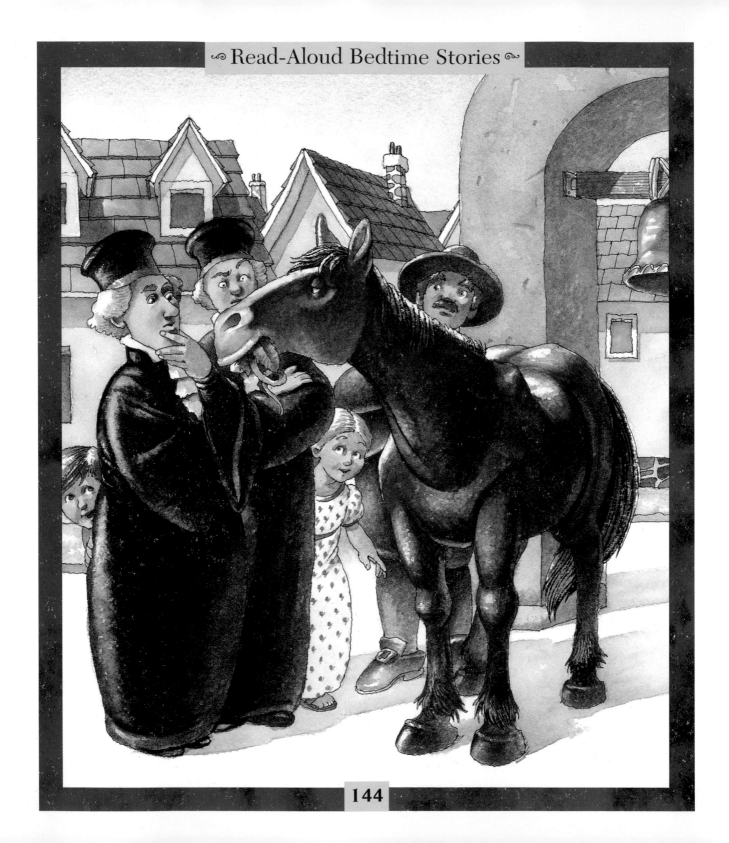

The mayor heard the Bell of Justice ringing. He put on his robe. He called to his assistant.

"Justice must be served," he said.

The mayor and his assistant went to the town square. All the people in town had gathered there. They wanted to find out who had been wronged.

The horse was so hungry. He kept pulling the vine. He did not notice all the people watching him.

The bell kept ringing.

The mayor stepped up to the horse. He gently placed his hand on the horse's thin back. The horse was startled. He suddenly saw all the people watching him.

"I know this horse," the mayor said.

"He belongs to the old knight," the mayor's assistant said.

"This is a noble steed," one man said. "He served the old knight well."

"He carried him through many fierce battles," an old woman said.

"He was always brave and loyal," another woman said.

"But look at him now," a little girl said. "He is just a hungry old horse without a home."

The mayor thought for a moment.

"This horse has been wronged," he said. "He deserves justice. Send for the knight at once."

The knight was brought to the square.

The mayor looked at him sadly.

"Honorable knight," the mayor said. "This horse served you well when you were both young. He is old now, but you turned him away. You let him go to find food and shelter. But you have plenty of money."

"Hear! Hear!" the townspeople said.

"You have done wrong," the mayor said.

"Hear! Hear!" the townspeople said.

"I hereby decree that you must pay for it," the mayor said. "We will provide this horse with food and shelter. Your gold will pay for his care."

"Hip! Hip! Hooray!" the townspeople said.

Justice had been served.

The knight gave up a pile of his gold. He did feel bad about the horse. He was glad the horse would have whatever he needed.

The townspeople built a stable for him. They took turns giving him food and water. The children loved to give him treats. He especially liked carrots and sugar cubes.

The old horse was happy for the rest of his days. He was glad he found the town and the good people. He was glad he had a new home. He was glad he had people who loved him.

He was especially glad for that tasty vine.

Stone Soup

Adapted by Lisa Harkrader ■ Illustrated by Barbara Lanza

A traveling man walked along a dirt road. He had a feather in his hat. He had a smile on his face.

His name was Jack Grand, and he was a Rat-a-tat man. That meant he could do all sorts of things. He could tumble. He could dance. He could walk on his hands. He could yodel. He could hum. He could play the drum. He could sing. He could whittle. He even knew some riddles.

He could do many things. He had a good life. But sometimes, he went hungry. He was hungry now. He had not eaten in many days.

"There must be something to eat around here," he said. "A wild onion or some walnuts or a dry old apple."

He searched the fields beside the road. He did not find anything to eat.

"Only rocks," he said.

He continued down the road. He walked up hills and through valleys. He walked and walked. He walked until he came to a village.

"Where there is a village, there are people. Where there are people, there is food. Maybe someone will feed a hungry traveling man," he said.

Jack ran to the village. He ran to the first house. A name was painted on the gate: TUBBS. He knocked on the door. An old man opened it. Jack swooped his hat from his head. He bowed low to the ground.

"May I help you?" asked the old man.

"Hello, Mr. Tubbs," Jack said. "I'm Jack Grand, the Rat-a-tat Man. I can tumble. I can dance. I can walk on my hands."

"I am sorry," said Mr. Tubbs. "I have no money for a rat-a-tat man."

"I understand," Jack said. "The truth is, I'm hungry. I'll do a few tricks to pay for a meal."

"I have nothing to share," said Mr. Tubbs. "I have only a bit of salt and pepper. Ask Miss Grubbs next door."

Jack hurried to the next house. He knocked on the door.

A thin woman answered. Jack swooped his hat from his head. He bowed low to the ground.

"May I help you?" asked the thin woman.

"Hello, Miss Grubbs," he said. "I'm Jack Grand, the Rat-a-tat Man. I can yodel. I can hum. I can play the drum."

"I'm sorry," said Miss Grubbs. "I have no money for a rat-a-tat man."

"I understand," Jack said. "The truth is, I'm hungry. I'll do a few tricks to pay for a meal."

"I have nothing to share," said Miss Grubbs. "I have only a head of garlic. Ask Mrs. Chubbs next door."

Jack hurried to the next house. He knocked on the door.

A plump woman answered. Jack swooped his hat from his head. He bowed low to the ground.

"May I help you?" asked the plump woman.

"Hello, Mrs. Chubbs," Jack said. "I'm Jack Grand, the Rat-a-tat Man. I can sing. I can whittle. I can even tell some riddles."

"I'm sorry," said Mrs. Chubbs. "I have no money for a rat-a-tat man."

"I understand," Jack said. "The truth is, I'm hungry. I'll do a few tricks to pay for a meal."

"I have nothing to share," said Mrs. Chubbs. "I have only a few potatoes. Ask someone else."

Jack did. He knocked on every door in the village. He swooped his hat from his head. He bowed low to the ground.

Nobody had enough food to share.

One woman had only cabbage. Her neighbor had only a few carrots. One family had only some bacon. Another family had only a handful of beans.

Jack sighed and set off down the road. He walked along for a while. He no longer had a smile on his face. He was too hungry to smile. He decided to sit down and rest.

He saw a stone.

It was not like the other stones in the road. It was smooth and white and round. It gave Jack an idea.

He picked it up and examined it.

"Perfect," he said.

He was happy again. He was so happy he ran back to town. He knocked on the first door in the village. Mr. Tubbs answered.

"I know you have no food to share," Jack said. "Do you have a big pot I could borrow?"

"A big pot?" asked Mr. Tubbs.

Jack nodded. He held up the smooth, white stone.

"What have you got there?" asked Mr. Tubbs.

"It's a soup stone," Jack said.

"A soup stone?" asked Mr. Tubbs.

Jack nodded again.

"It makes great soup," he said. "I just add water."

Mr. Tubbs went inside. He came back with a big pot.

Jack carried the big pot to the village square. He filled it with water. He built a fire underneath it. He dropped the stone into it.

The pot bubbled and brewed. Jack waited and waited. He waited as long as he could. Then he dipped his spoon into the water. He tasted it.

"Perfect," he said.

"It's good?" asked Mr. Tubbs.

"Yes," said Jack. "It's very good. It would only be better if. . ."

Mr. Tubbs leaned in closer.

"If what?" he asked.

"Well," said Jack. "It would only be better with a little salt and pepper. Not much. Just a little. Oh, well. The soup will be just fine without it."

"Salt and pepper?" Mr. Tubbs asked.

"Yes," Jack said. "Don't worry, though. The soup will still be good."

"I have salt and pepper," said Mr. Tubbs.

"You do?" said Jack.

"Yes!" said Mr. Tubbs.

He ran to his cottage as fast as he could. He returned with a salt shaker and a pepper mill.

Jack sprinkled the salt into the pot. He ground the pepper into the pot. He stirred.

The pot bubbled and brewed. Jack waited and waited. He waited as long as he could. Then he dipped his spoon into the pot. He tasted the soup.

"Perfect," he said.

Miss Grubbs came out of her cottage. She had been watching Jack. She came over and peeked into the pot.

"It's stone soup," said Mr. Tubbs.

"Is it good?" asked Miss Grubbs.

"Yes," said Jack. "It's very good. It would only be better if. . ."

Miss Grubbs leaned in closer.

"If what?" she asked.

"Well," said Jack. "It would only be better with a little garlic. Not much. Just a little. Oh, well. The soup will be fine without it."

"Garlic?" Miss Grubbs asked.

"Yes," Jack said. "Don't worry, though. The soup will still be good."

"I have garlic," said Miss Grubbs.

"You do?" said Jack.

"Yes!" said Miss Grubbs.

She ran to her cottage as fast as she could. She returned with a beautiful head of garlic.

Jack chopped the head of garlic. He sprinkled the chopped garlic into the pot and stirred.

The pot bubbled and brewed. Jack waited and waited. He waited as long as he could. Then he dipped his spoon into the pot. He tasted the soup.

"Perfect," he said.

Mrs. Chubbs came out of her cottage. She had been watching Jack, too. She came over and peeked into the pot.

"It's stone soup," said Miss Grubbs.

"Is it good?" asked Mrs. Chubbs.

"Yes," said Jack. "It's very good. It would only be better if. . ."

Mrs. Chubbs leaned in closer.

"If what?" she asked.

"Well," said Jack. "It would only be better with a few potatoes. Not many. Just a few. Oh, well. The soup will be fine without them."

"Potatoes?" Mrs. Chubbs asked.

"Yes," Jack said. "Don't worry, though. The soup will still be good."

"I have potatoes," said Mrs. Chubbs.

"You do?" said Jack.

"Yes!" said Mrs. Chubbs.

She ran to her cottage as fast as she could. She returned with her apron full of potatoes.

Jack peeled and sliced the potatoes. He dropped the slices into the pot and stirred.

The pot bubbled and brewed. Jack waited and waited. He waited as long as he could. Then he dipped his spoon into the pot. He tasted the soup.

"Perfect," he said.

By this time, the entire village had gathered around Jack. They had been watching from their windows. They all wanted to know what was in the pot. They were very curious.

"It's stone soup," said Mrs. Chubbs.

"Is it good?" they asked.

"Yes," said Jack. "It's very good. It would only be better if we had. . ."

"If we had what?" asked the villagers.

"Cabbage," said Jack.

A woman ran to get cabbage.

"Carrots," said Jack.

A man ran to get carrots.

"A bit of bacon," said Jack, "and some beans."

The villagers ran to get the food. Jack threw it all into the pot and stirred. The pot bubbled and brewed. Jack could hardly wait. He dipped his spoon into the soup and tasted it.

"Perfect," he said.

"It's good?" everyone asked at once.

"Yes," said Jack, "and it's done."

Jack spooned soup out for everyone. He ate until he was full. The villagers ate until they were full. Everyone ate until the pot was empty.

Empty, that is, except for the smooth, white stone.

"Use it for your next pot of stone soup," Jack said to the villagers.

Then he did his tricks. He tumbled. He danced. He walked on his hands. He yodeled. He hummed. He played a drum. He sang. He whittled. He even told some riddles. When he was done, he waved to the villagers.

He walked for a while. Then he sat down to rest. He saw a rock. It was shiny and black. He picked it up and put it in his pocket.

"It's perfect," he said, "for making rock stew."

Jack and the Beanstalk

Adapted by Joanna Spathis ▪ Illustrated by Susan Spellman

*J*ack and his mother lived in a small country house. They were very poor. They did not have enough food to eat.

Jack's mother was sad. She remembered when there was plenty of food. They used to have a warm home. Jack used to have toys. Jack's father worked hard to give them things. But Jack's father was killed by a greedy giant. The giant stole everything they had.

"Son, you must go to town tomorrow," Jack's mother said. "It is time to sell our old cow."

The next morning, Jack led the cow into town.

"Your cow is just too skinny," the butcher said.

"Your cow is too old to milk," a farmer said.

No one wanted the cow. Then an old man walked up to Jack.

"What a perfect cow!" the old man said. "I will give you five beans for such a fine cow."

Jack looked at the five small beans and frowned.

"They are magic beans," the old man said. "Plant the beans. Your family will eat like royalty."

Jack skipped home with the five magic beans. He proudly showed his mother, but she only cried. She threw the beans into their dry garden. They went to bed hungry again.

That night, the beans grew, and grew, and grew!

A beautiful beanstalk stood in the garden in the morning. The thick plant grew straight into the sky. Jack's mother picked lots of plump beans.

"We will have a wonderful bean soup," she said.

Jack had other ideas. He wanted to climb the tall beanstalk into the clouds. He put one foot on the beanstalk and pulled himself up.

"Be careful," Jack's mother said, "and don't be late for supper!"

Jack climbed and climbed. The houses of the town looked small when he looked down. They were as small as toys. He climbed some more.

"I just want to touch a cloud," he thought.

As he climbed through the cloud, Jack saw a castle. He rubbed his eyes. The castle was huge. It was bigger than anything he had ever imagined. The road to the castle was paved in gold.

"I am so cold and thirsty!" Jack thought. "I will go to the castle."

Jack knocked at the door. He knocked again and again. The heavy door finally opened. A very tall woman looked around. She did not see Jack because he was so small.

"Hello!" Jack yelled. "Down here!"

"Oh, my! Look what we have here," the tall woman said.

"I am very cold and thirsty," Jack said.

"Please come inside," the tall woman said.

She gently picked Jack up and took him inside.

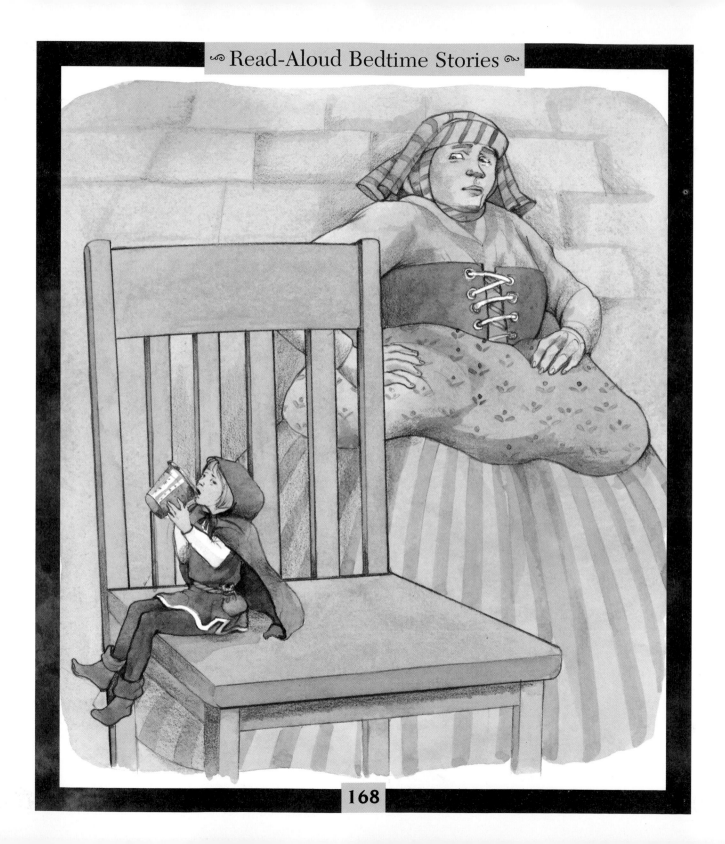

She bundled Jack in her handkerchief. She gave him a thimble of tea.

"You must be very quiet," she said. "My husband has a terrible temper. A very terrible temper. He is a giant, you know."

Jack gasped. He knew all about the giant. He was very frightened.

Suddenly, Jack felt the floor shake. A cake in the oven fell. Jack heard loud footsteps. He hid behind a bowl of fruit on the table.

"Fee-fi-fo-fum! I smell a little boy!" the giant yelled.

"Don't be silly," the giant's wife said. "It is just your supper that you smell. Sit and eat."

The giant's wife placed a large plate of food on the table.

The giant ate his supper in two huge swallows. He ate a whole loaf of bread. He wiped his beard on his sleeve when he was finished.

"Bring me my hen," the giant said.

The giant's wife brought in a hen. Jack could not believe his eyes. The magic hen had belonged to his father. Jack knew it laid eggs of pure gold. Jack watched as the hen laid her eggs. The giant laughed and demanded more eggs. Jack was no longer afraid. He was angry.

The giant finally had enough eggs. He leaned back in his chair and fell asleep. He snored loudly.

Jack jumped from the table. He grabbed the hen and ran from the castle. He climbed down the beanstalk as fast as he could.

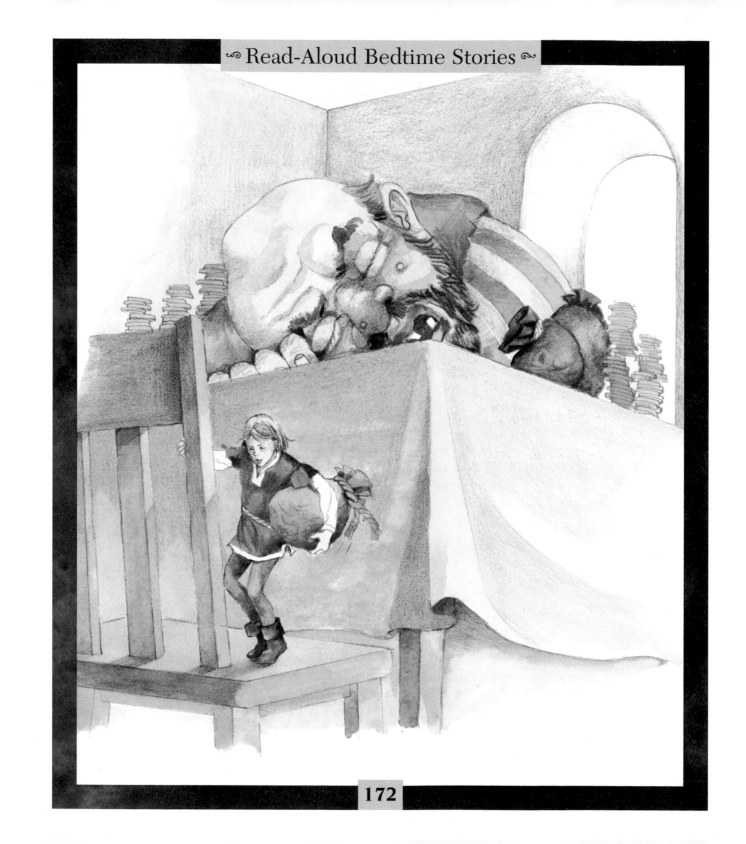

Jack watched the giant count his bags of coins. Jack knew the coins had belonged to his father. Jack became angrier and angrier at the ugly giant.

The giant soon grew tired of counting. His head fell on the table with a loud thump. He began to snore.

The giant's snore shook the whole kitchen. Jack jumped out of the sugar bowl. He ran across the table. He grabbed a bag of coins. He climbed down from the table and ran.

He ran and ran. He ran as fast as his legs could carry him. He ran for the beanstalk. He climbed through the clouds and found his way home.

His mother was waiting for him.

"Jack, you are late again," she said. "I was very worried. I made a nice stew for you. It is cold now."

"I have another surprise for you," Jack said.

Jack handed his mother the bag of coins.

"Jack!" his mother said. "It is a miracle! We have more than we need now. It is time to cut down the beanstalk."

"Not yet," Jack said. "We do not have everything yet."

"We do," she said. "We have plenty for our neighbors as well."

"Tomorrow, I will climb one last time," Jack said.

"One last time," she said. "Then I will cut it down myself."

"Okay," Jack said. "It will be my last climb."

In the morning, Jack climbed the beanstalk again. He climbed and climbed. He climbed his way through the clouds.

He walked up the gold road to the castle. The giant's wife had left the kitchen window open. Jack climbed through it. He hid behind a heavy curtain.

The giant's wife hummed softly. Jack waited patiently.

Suddenly, Jack heard the giant's footsteps. The windows shook. A teacup fell off the table. All the curtains swayed.

"Could you please walk more softly?" the giant's wife asked.

The giant sniffed at the air.

"Fee-fi-fo-fum! I smell a little boy!" the giant yelled.

The giant's wife checked in the oven. She looked behind the bowl of fruit. She did not see a little boy.

"You smell these meat pies," she said. "It is time to eat."

The giant ate the six meat pies in six bites.

"Bring me my harp," the giant said.

Jack knew the harp belonged to his father. Jack's mother had told him stories about it. It was a magic harp. It had the most beautiful sound.

"Play," the giant said.

The harp played. The giant's eyes grew heavy. He started to snore. The snoring blew the curtains back.

Jack climbed onto the table. He grabbed the harp.

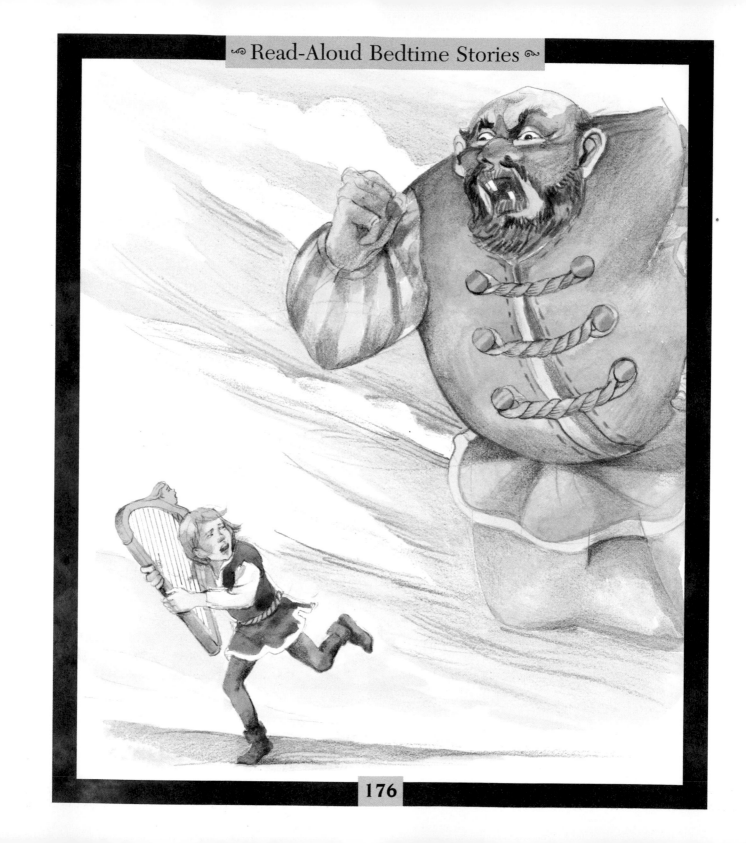

The harp shrieked. It was not used to being interrupted. The shrieks woke the giant. The giant yelled as he rose from the table.

"Why are you raising your voice?" the giant's wife asked.

"That boy has my harp!" the giant yelled.

Jack jumped from the table. He ran with the harp. He ran beneath the table. He ran between the chairs.

The giant smashed the table with his heavy fists. He pushed the chairs aside. He tried to grab Jack.

Jack was too quick. He jumped through the open window. He ran down the golden road. He ran and ran. He ran faster than he ever had before.

"Come back with my harp!" the giant yelled.

The giant took huge steps, but he was still slow. He had trouble seeing Jack because Jack was so small. The giant's footsteps shook the clouds and made it rain.

Jack finally reached the beanstalk. He climbed down as quickly as he could. The giant was close behind him. The giant shook the beanstalk. Jack held on as it swayed back and forth.

Jack could see his mother on the ground. He was late again!

"I made you a warm supper. It is cold now!" his mother said.

Jack jumped off the beanstalk.

"I will cut the beanstalk down," she said. "I told you I would."

Jack's mother was very upset. She did not know the giant was climbing down the beanstalk.

"Mother, chop it down!" Jack said.

"I will, then," she said. "I told you to be careful. You came down the beanstalk much too fast."

"Hurry, Mother!" Jack said.

Jack pointed toward the sky.

His mother looked up into the clouds. She saw the beanstalk swaying. Then she saw a giant pair of boots!

She struck the beanstalk with an ax. It began to fall over.

The magic beanstalk crashed to the ground. The giant crashed down with the beanstalk.

Jack and his mother celebrated with all their neighbors. They had a great feast. They danced to the lovely songs of the harp.

Jack walked to town the next morning. He bought his mother a healthy new cow.

"Son, I am proud of you," his mother said.

She was happy again. That made Jack happy, too.

They lived happily. They had plenty to eat. Their home was warm and cozy. Jack had toys again.

They would not see the giant ever again.

Rip Van Winkle

Adapted by Brian Conway ■ Illustrated by John Lund

The Catskill Mountains are a magical place. They are a wild place. They are a place filled with many beautiful sights. Clear brooks run down the hills. Valleys spread out wide. Stone cliffs rise up to the sky. Tall trees reach into the clouds.

The mountains are filled with legends, too. The mountain people tell the legends like amazing stories. They seem too strange to be true. One can never be sure.

One story might be true. It is about a man named Rip Van Winkle.

Rip lived in a town in the foothills. He was a friendly man. He always had a smile for anyone he met. He greeted everybody with a wave and a tip of his hat. Everyone loved him.

The children in town especially loved him. They followed him wherever he went.

"Give us piggyback rides, Mr. Van Winkle," they said.

Rip always did. He played games with them, too. He flew kites with them. He shot marbles with them. He even jumped rope with them.

Even the neighborhood dogs loved Rip. They never barked when he passed by. They wagged their tails when he petted them.

Rip Van Winkle was a wonderful neighbor. He could never turn down a neighbor who asked for help. He always helped his neighbors with their chores. He loved to help.

Rip had just one fault. He did not like to do his chores.

He helped his neighbors with their chores. He loved to help. He just did not like to do his own chores.

That made everyone happy except his wife.

His fences always fell over. The weeds in his yard always grew fast and wild. His cow was always running away. His pigs were always trampling through the garden.

Rip's children were as raggedy as his farm. Their clothes were always torn. Their faces were always dirty. They ran around without shoes. They did not like to do their chores either.

Young Rip was the worst of all. He never listened to anybody. He never did what was asked of him. He was just like his father.

"Young Rip is going to turn out just like his father," the neighbors said.

Rip's wife was never very happy with either of them.

"I thought you were going to fix the fence today," she said.

"It's a very big fence," Rip said.

"Get Young Rip to help you," she said.

Rip called for his son, but Young Rip didn't come.

He decided to leave the fence until tomorrow. He called for his dog, Wolf. He waved to his daughter, Judith.

He headed for the mountains.

Rip and his dog spent a lot of time in the mountains. Rip liked to go fishing. Wolf liked to hunt for squirrels.

Some days, they just walked.

"I have had a busy day," Rip said.

Wolf wagged his tail as Rip petted him.

"Let's find a place where there are no fences around," he said.

They walked up one of the tall mountains. Half way up, Rip sat down and enjoyed the view. Wolf sat next to him.

Rip and Wolf passed the whole afternoon that way.

"It's getting late," Rip said. "We should get home."

Rip stood up. He heard someone call his name. He did not see anyone. There was no one around.

"Rip Van Winkle," a voice said.

Rip turned around. He saw a strange little man. He carried a huge barrel on his shoulder.

"Would you help me with this?" the little man asked.

The little man was strange. But Rip could not refuse anyone who asked for help.

"Of course," Rip said. "I would love to help."

He took the barrel from the strange little man. He climbed up the mountain after him.

Rip heard loud claps and crashes as they climbed. It sounded like thunder. Rip looked around. There was not a cloud in the clear sky.

"There must be a storm on the other side of the mountain," Rip said.

The little man just smiled. He led Rip and Wolf through a crack in a cliff. There was a clearing inside.

There was a group in the clearing. Many strange little men were gathered there. Rip stared at them.

"I have lived in these mountains all my life," he thought. "I have never seen such strange little men before."

Rip saw something even more unusual as they got closer. The strange little men were bowling.

Every time the ball hit the pins, there was a crash. The sound echoed through the mountains. It sounded like thunder!

The little men stopped bowling when they saw Rip and Wolf.

"Thank you, neighbor," one strange little man said.

He took the barrel from Rip. He poured a dark liquid from it. The strange little men passed around cups and drank.

They offered a cup to Rip. He drank the dark liquid. It was very tasty. He asked for more.

He drank several cups and started to feel tired. His eyes drooped. His head felt heavy. He drifted off to sleep.

It was late when Rip woke up. The sun was shining high in the sky. It was almost the afternoon.

He was no longer in the clearing. He was back where he had met the first little man.

"I have been here all night," he said. "Mrs. Van Winkle is going to be very upset with me."

He whistled for his dog. Wolf did not come running.

"Maybe Wolf ran home," he said. "I should do the same thing."

Rip's knees cracked when he stood up. His legs were stiff.

"Sleeping outside isn't good for me," he said. "My legs feel like they belong to an old man."

He started down the hill.

He had dreamed about strange little men. He remembered his dream as he walked. The dream had seemed so real. He felt confused.

Rip walked into town. The people he saw did not look familiar. He did not know anyone. They did not seem to know him.

The townspeople stared at Rip. He smiled. He waved. He tipped his hat. Some of the people laughed. Others looked the other way.

Finally, Rip looked down. He saw why everyone had been staring at him. He had a long gray beard!

Now, reality seemed like a dream.

Rip's beard had grown down to his knees. It was gray and white. It was knotted and tangled.

His clothes were ripped and tattered. He was dirty. He looked like a crazy old man.

Children raced up to Rip.

"Who are you, old man?" one boy asked.

"What are you doing in our town?" asked another.

Rip was more confused than ever.

He walked through town. The people were different. The buildings were different. The dogs ran after him and barked.

"I'd better get home," Rip said. "Things will be all right once I see my wife and children."

But Rip got lost on the way to his house. The paths and roads were no longer the same.

After some time, Rip found his farmhouse. It did not look at all like it did the day before. The fence had fallen to the ground. Weeds grew all over. The roof was falling in. The front door was swinging on its hinges.

Rip waited for his wife and children to appear. No one moved around the house. No one came out. The swinging door creaked in the breeze.

Rip walked slowly toward the house. It was dark and dirty inside. Nobody had lived there in a very long time.

Rip ran back to town. He wanted to find something familiar. He wanted to find someone who remembered him.

He thought he could find his friends at the inn. But the inn was not where it used to be. There was a schoolhouse there, instead.

A man dressed in a fine suit walked up to Rip.

"What are you doing here?" he asked.

"I am looking for someone who remembers me," Rip said.

"Did you used to live around here?" the man asked.

Rip did not know what to say.

"I asked you a question," the man said.

"I know," Rip said. "I just don't know how to answer."

"It's a simple question," the man said. "Did you used to live here?"

"Yes," Rip said. "I lived here yesterday."

"I don't know what you are up to," the man said.

"I'm not trying to start a fight," Rip said. "I am a kind person. My name is Rip Van Winkle."

"Rip Van Winkle?" the man asked. "I know Rip, and you're not him. That's Rip Van Winkle over there."

The man pointed to a tree in the park. There was a young man standing under it.

He looked like Rip had looked yesterday.

Then a woman and her family walked up to Rip. They wanted to meet the old, bearded stranger.

"Hello," the woman said. "I am Judith Gardener. These are my children."

The children were afraid of the stranger. Rip leaned forward to look at Judith's face. Something was very familiar about it.

"What is your father's name?" he asked.

"Rip Van Winkle was his name," she said. "I have not seen him in twenty years."

"What became of him?" Rip asked.

She sighed. Tears sprang from her eyes.

"He walked up into the mountains one day," she said. "He never came back. His dog came home without him. We have not heard anything about him since."

A tear formed in his eye, too.

"And what about your mother?" Rip asked.

"She passed away a few months ago," Judith said.

Rip began to cry. His wife was gone. His children had grown. He had missed twenty years of his life!

"Are you all right, sir?" Judith asked.

"Please don't call me sir," Rip said. "Don't you recognize me? Don't you know who I am? I am your father!"

Young Rip and Judith had always wanted to see their father again. But they still did not believe Rip's story.

"I fell asleep on the mountain," he said. "Now everything has changed. Doesn't anyone know me?"

Young Rip liked to help. He went to find the tailor's wife. She was the oldest woman in town. If she did not know the stranger, nobody would.

The old woman looked into old Rip's eyes. She squinted.

"Sure enough," she said. "I'd know him anywhere. Welcome home, Rip Van Winkle."

Rip smiled.

He told his family about the little men. He told them about the clearing in the mountains.

The whole town gathered to hear Rip's story.

He told the people about the little men's game. He told them about the strange liquid he drank. He told them about his very long nap.

"When I woke up," he said, "it was twenty years later! My life passed by in one night!"

Everyone was glad to have old Rip Van Winkle back.

His story became a legend. The sound of thunder in the Catskill Mountains makes people talk. They say it is Rip's strange little friends bowling on the mountain tops.

The Flying Prince

Adapted by Jennifer Boudart ■ Illustrated by Kathi Ember

*P*rince Rashar lived in a big castle. He had horses to ride. He had fine clothes to wear. He had servants to sing and dance for him. He had guards to protect him. But the prince was lonely. He did not have any true friends.

The prince spent his days riding alone across his kingdom. One morning, he entered a strange forest. A parrot landed on a tree above him.

"Who are you?" asked the parrot.

"I am Prince Rashar," said the prince.

"Just a prince?" asked the parrot. "I am a king. The King of the Parrots!"

"Do all the birds in this forest talk?" asked the prince.

"Oh, no! I am the only one," said the parrot. "Saledra gave me this power. She wished for someone to talk to."

"Who is Saledra?" asked the prince.

"Saledra is a beautiful and kind princess," said the parrot. "She is also very lonely. I am one of her only friends."

"I would like to meet this princess," said the prince.

"You cannot," said the bird. "As her friend, I must protect her. You might want to hurt her."

The prince wanted to say he would never do that.

"You could not find her anyway," said the parrot.

The prince watched the parrot fly away.

Prince Rashar had been lucky enough to find the parrot. Maybe his luck would lead him to the princess. He decided to keep riding.

It became dark. He spotted a campfire. He had entered a trolls' camp. He saw four trolls, and they were fighting.

"What is the trouble?" asked the prince.

"We were digging for mushrooms," said the first troll. "We found these magical things instead. Let us show you."

"This rug flies anywhere you wish to go," said the second troll.

"This bag gives whatever you wish for," said the third troll.

"This rope wraps around whatever it touches," said the fourth troll.

The trolls were fighting over who should get the treasures. Prince Rashar thought about it. He knew trolls were very greedy. He knew they loved a good contest. He also knew they were hard to fool.

He quickly came up with a plan.

"I will shoot an arrow into the forest," he said. "Whoever brings it back first will get to keep everything."

The prince shot an arrow from his bow. The greedy trolls took off to find it. The prince did not wait to see who came back first. He had fooled them.

He placed the bag and the rope on the rug. He sat on the rug. He told his horse to return to the castle.

"Take me to Princess Saledra," said the prince to the rug.

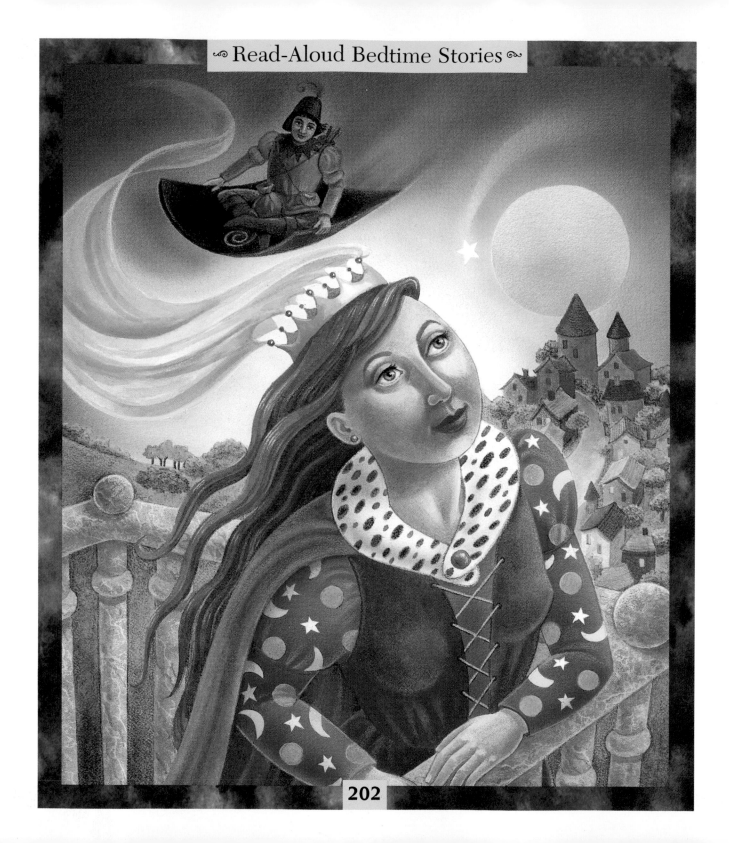

The prince flew all day without stopping. He watched new lands pass by below. The rug flew over forests, rivers, farms, and towns.

The rug sailed into a wall of clouds. They covered the prince like a white blanket. He no longer knew where or how fast he was going. He lost track of time and fell asleep.

He woke up to find himself on the ground. He wondered if he was in Princess Saledra's kingdom. He took his things and started walking. He soon reached the edge of a city. There was a gatekeeper in front of the city gate.

"I need to see Princess Saledra right away," the prince said.

"You can see her castle up on that hill," said the gatekeeper. "You must wait to see her. She does not leave the castle during the day."

The prince was nervous about meeting the princess. He wondered why. He was a prince himself! He had talked to a parrot. He had fooled four trolls. He had flown on a magic rug. There was nothing to be nervous about.

"I could be a good friend," thought the prince.

He waited. The sun set and the moon came out.

Someone walked out on the castle roof. The prince hoped it was the princess. He flew up on his rug for a closer look.

It was too dark to see very much. A woman raised her hand. Sparks of light flew from her fingertips. They became stars that shone upon the castle. Their light was brighter than the sun. They lit the face of Princess Saledra.

Prince Rashar knew the woman was Princess Saledra. He could see right away she was kind. But her eyes looked very sad. She did not know he was floating above her.

"I have powerful magic," the princess said to herself. "But it cannot give me what I wish for most. I wish I had just one true friend."

She raised her hand again. One by one, the stars fell from the sky. They dropped into her waiting palm. She turned and went inside. The night became cold and dark.

Prince Rashar thought about Princess Saledra's words. He wished for a friend, too. Maybe he could become her friend. But how?

"I will leave the princess a gift!" thought the prince. "I will wait to see if she likes it. If she does, I will go to meet her."

The prince landed his rug on the roof. He took out his magic bag.

"Bag, give me a silk robe," he said. "Make it a perfect match for the gown the princess wore."

Prince Rashar reached inside the bag. The robe was there!

The prince quietly opened the door on the roof. He tiptoed into Princess Saledra's royal bedroom. She was asleep on a big bed.

"You even look sad when you sleep," he said. "I hope this will make you smile. I hope it will make you happy."

The prince laid the robe on the bed and left.

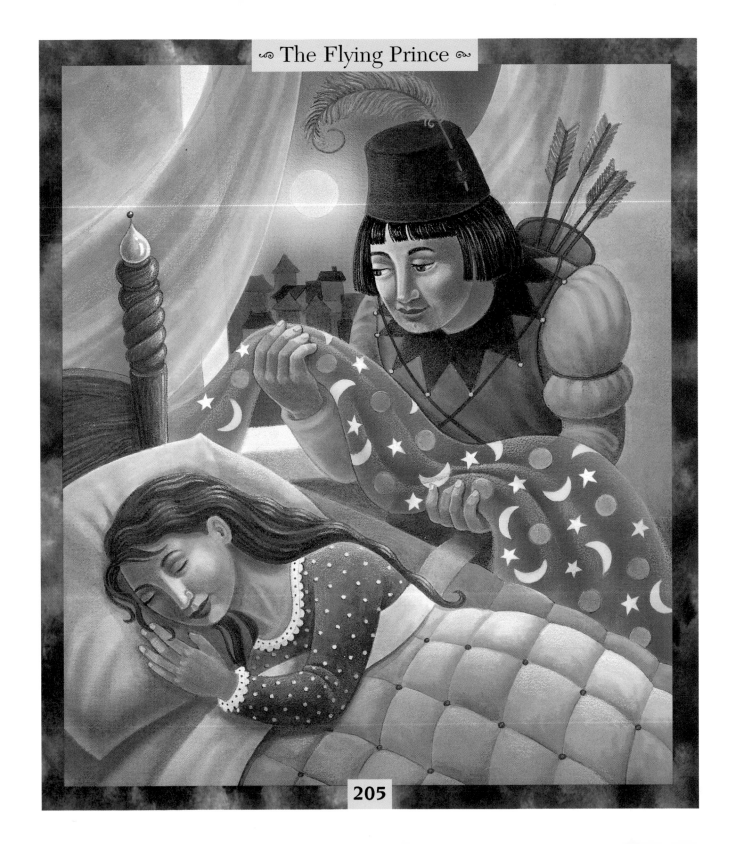

Prince Rashar took Princess Saledra to see his rug. She asked for a ride. They flew into the night together.

They did not return until morning.

"I wish you could stay in my kingdom," said the princess.

"I do, too. But I have my own kingdom," said the prince.

"I will miss you," said the princess.

"I will miss you, too" said the prince.

Prince Rashar thought about his magical things. They gave him an idea. He whispered a wish into his magic bag. He pulled out two mirrors.

"These are magic mirrors," said the prince. "Mine will show me what you are doing when I look into it."

"Mine will show me what you are doing," said the princess.

"We can visit each other whenever we are lonely," said the prince.

"How will I know when you are lonely?" asked the princess.

"Come if you see a flower in my hat," said the prince.

"Come if you see a flower in my hair," said the princess. "But I do not have a way to get to your kingdom."

The prince whispered into his magic bag again. He pulled out a flying rug just like his own. Nothing could keep them apart.

"You are a true friend, Rashar!" said the princess.

"You are a true friend, too, Saledra," said the prince.

Adapted by Lisa Harkrader ■ Illustrated by Tammie Lyon

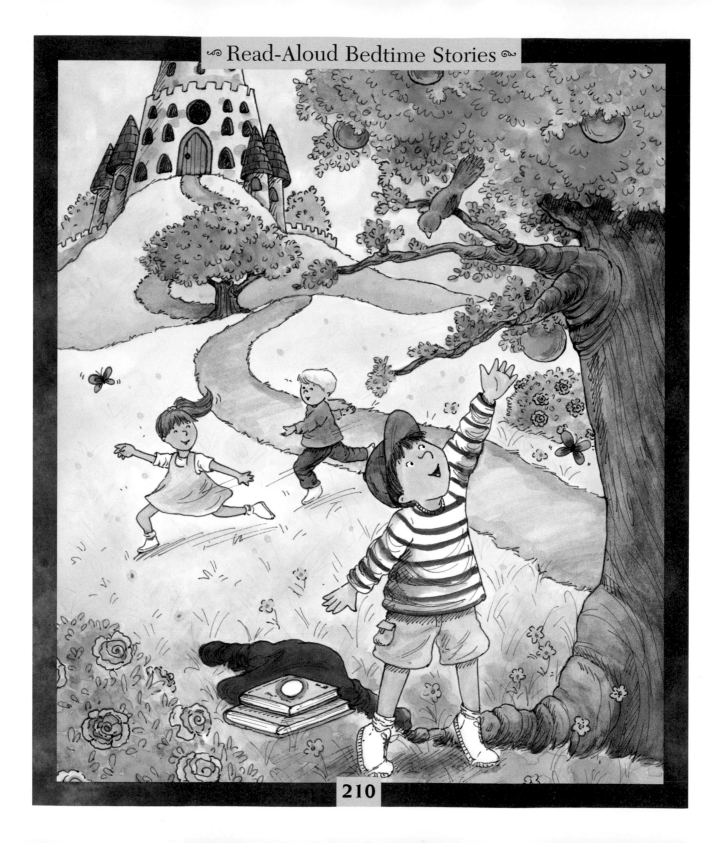

*J*acob ran behind his friends. His feet crunched through fallen leaves. His schoolbooks jostled in his arms.

"Wait for me," he called.

He raced to catch up with Matthew and Rachel. They were taking him to the castle on the hill. He had never been there before.

They stopped at the edge of town. Jacob looked up. The castle towered above them. It was big and gray and gloomy.

It was also empty. The windows were dark. The doors were bolted shut. Nobody lived there. The owner had been away for many years. He had been away for so long nobody remembered him.

But Jacob was not afraid of the gloomy castle. The lovely garden surrounding it was wonderful.

Late summer sun shone over the green grass. Butterflies flitted from flower to flower. Birds twittered in the trees. The leaves of the trees ruffled in the breeze.

Jacob, Matthew, and Rachel tossed their jackets and schoolbooks in the grass. Matthew and Rachel ran through the garden, playing tag.

Jacob did not want to play tag. He saw a tree in the corner of the garden. Hanging from each branch were ripe golden peaches.

He ran to the tree. He stretched. He jumped. He tried to reach a peach.

"What do you think you're doing?" a booming voice asked.

Jacob turned around. An enormous man was standing inside the gate. He was a giant! His legs were like tree trunks. His feet were like boats. His chest was like a barrel. He was so tall his head brushed the tallest branches. He was so strong the ground shook when he walked.

He was very angry.

"Get out of my garden!" he yelled.

"Yes, sir!" Matthew and Rachel said.

Matthew and Rachel scrambled through the grass. They grabbed their jackets and schoolbooks. They ran past the giant. They went through the gate. They ran from the garden.

Jacob just stared at the giant.

"Your garden?" he asked. "Nobody lives here."

The giant stared back.

"I live here. I went away. I'm back. This is my castle and my garden. I don't need wild children ruining it."

"We're not ruining anything," Jacob said. "We're not wild. It's so wonderful here. We were just playing."

"It's mine!" yelled the giant. "Get out!"

"You're just, you're just. . .selfish!" Jacob said.

He snatched his jacket and schoolbooks from the grass. He looked at the giant for a minute. Then he ran from the garden.

Jacob, Matthew, and Rachel stayed far away from the castle after that. Autumn turned to winter, and winter turned to spring. Jacob and his friends played in the schoolyard. They played in the park. They played in their own yards at home.

It was not the same.

"It's not like playing in the castle garden," Jacob said.

"Maybe the giant will go away again," Matthew said.

"Maybe he's already gone," Rachel said.

"We should go and look," Jacob said. "He can't be mad at us for looking."

Jacob and his friends ran to the castle. It was still big and gray and gloomy. The windows were still dark.

But they could no longer see the garden. The giant had built a stone wall around it. On the wall was a sign. It read:

KEEP OUT!

ESPECIALLY CHILDREN

"The giant is still here," Matthew said.

"It doesn't look like he'll ever go away," Rachel said.

"Let's look over the wall," Jacob said.

A pile of firewood was stacked against the wall. They climbed onto it and peeked over the wall.

What they saw made them gasp.

"Oh, no!" said Jacob.

He and Matthew and Rachel stared at the garden.

Snow covered the grass. A cold wind whistled. The trees were bare. The branches stood crooked and black against the sky.

Jacob shook his head.

"What happened?" he asked. "Why hasn't winter gone from the garden? Why hasn't spring come?"

"Maybe it's just taking longer this year," Matthew said.

"Maybe the flowers will start to bloom soon," Rachel said.

Each day, Jacob, Matthew, and Rachel ran to the castle. Each day, they stood on the pile of firewood. Each day, they peeked over the wall. Each day, Jacob shook his head.

Outside of the garden, the days were becoming warmer. The sun was brighter. Flowers blossomed. Spring was turning to summer.

Inside of the garden, it was still winter. The flowers were not blossoming. The trees were not budding. Birds no longer twittered in the trees. Butterflies no longer flitted around.

Only one lone peach still hung on the peach tree. The other peaches had fallen to the ground. They poked up through the snow. They were shriveled and brown.

"It is no longer wonderful," Jacob said.

Jacob, Matthew, and Rachel kept watching the garden. Each day, it was the same. It was always winter.

One day, they saw the giant. He was leaning over a rosebush. A tiny rosebud was starting to bloom.

"Look!" Jacob said. "A flower."

"Maybe spring is finally coming to the garden," said Rachel.

The giant looked at the flower for a long time. He reached down to touch it. Its petals crumbled and fell to the ground.

The giant sighed and shook his head. He was still big. He was still strong. But he did not look angry anymore.

"He looks lonely," Jacob said.

"He should be lonely," Rachel said.

"He yelled at us," Matthew said.

"And chased us away," Rachel said.

"He just looks so sad," Jacob said. "We should help him."

"I'm not going to help him," Matthew said.

"I'm not going to help him, either," Rachel said.

Jacob watched the giant. The giant stared at his dead garden. He stared at the wilted flower and bare trees. He shook his head. He turned and went back into his castle.

"I'd help you," Jacob whispered, "if only I knew how."

Matthew and Rachel climbed down from the stack of firewood.

Jacob felt so sad. He took one last look at the garden. He turned to climb down, too.

He lost his balance. His foot slipped, and the firewood began to tumble down. He kicked at the wall. He tried to regain his balance. One of the stones moved when he kicked it.

"Look," said Jacob. "It's loose!"

Matthew and Rachel helped him move the stone. They wiggled it. They pushed it. They pulled it. They tugged it. The stone finally broke free with a loud pop.

All of them tumbled backward in the grass. They stared at the stone. They stared at the hole where the stone had been. The hole went all the way through the wall. It went all the way through to the garden!

"Should we go through?" Matthew asked.

"Yes," Rachel said. "Unless you're afraid."

"I'm not afraid," Matthew said. "Are you afraid?"

"I'm not afraid," said Rachel. "Are you afraid, Jacob?"

"No," Jacob said. "I'm not afraid."

"Good," said Rachel. "You can go first, then."

Jacob swallowed. He looked into the hole. He climbed into it. He crawled all the way through to the other side.

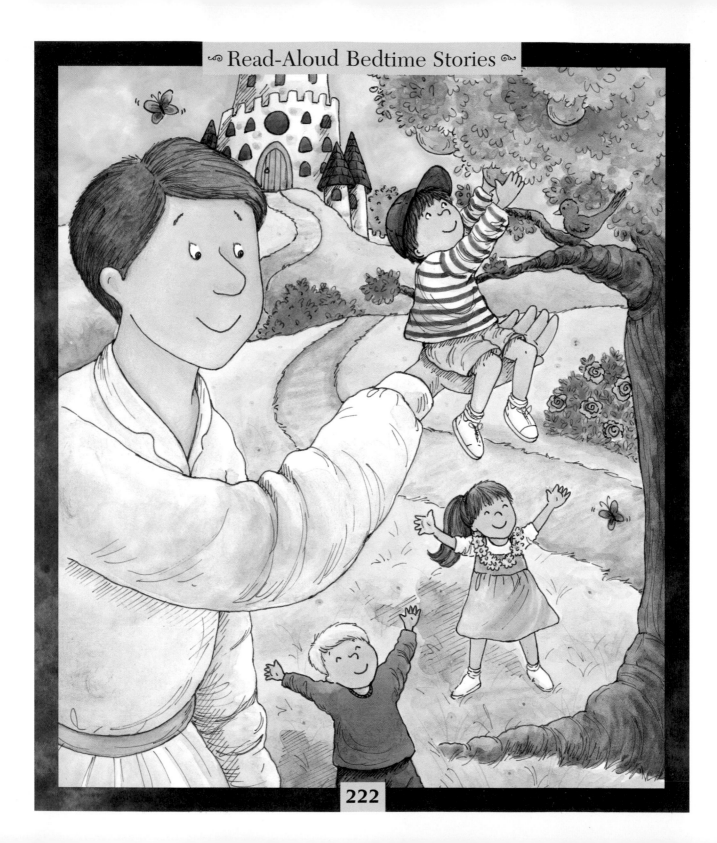

Jacob stepped into the garden. Matthew and Rachel followed.

Wind whistled through the trees. Snow swirled at their feet. Their breath came out in little white puffs. They shivered. They felt very sad.

"Maybe we should go back," Matthew said.

"The giant will yell at us again," Rachel said.

"I don't think he will," Jacob said.

"He will yell at us," Matthew said.

"We ruined his garden wall," Rachel said.

"No, he won't," Jacob said. "We'll stay here in the corner by the peach tree. The giant won't even see us. The tree limbs will hide us."

"Okay," Matthew said.

"But only for a little while," Rachel said.

Matthew and Rachel ran to make snow angels.

Jacob did not want to make snow angels. He stared at the peach tree. He stared at the lone peach. It hung from the highest branch.

He stretched. He jumped. He tried to reach the peach.

"You'll never get it like that," said a booming voice.

A huge hand picked him up from the ground. It lifted him to the highest branch of the tree.

Jacob turned around. He was staring straight into the eyes of the selfish giant.

"Oh!" said Jacob.

The giant smiled at him.

The giant lifted Jacob to the top of the tree. He held Jacob steady. Jacob reached up. He plucked the peach from the highest branch.

"Thank you," Jacob whispered.

"No," said the giant. "Thank you."

The giant pointed at the tree. New buds were popped out on the branches. They turned into leaves.

Jacob stared at them. He turned and stared at the garden.

The snow had melted where Rachel and Matthew were playing. Green grass grew beneath their feet. The sun broke through the clouds. Butterflies flitted across the grass. Birds twittered in the trees. Flowers popped up all over the garden.

"Spring has finally come!" Jacob said.

"Yes," the giant said. "You brought it. You brought joy to the garden and to me. The joy brought back the spring."

Jacob, Matthew, and Rachel went to the garden every day after that. They taught the giant to play tag. The giant lifted them up to pick peaches. They ate the peaches and chased the butterflies.

Summer came to the garden and then autumn and winter. But winter did not stay. The snow melted. The sun shone. Each year, spring returned.

✺ Prince Carrots ✺

Adapted by Jamie Elder ▪ Illustrated by Kathy Mitchell

225

There once was a time when there were many kings and queens. They had children. Their children were princes and princesses. One of these princes was Prince Carrots.

Prince Carrots was not very handsome. In fact, he was very hard to look at. His face was too wide. His nose was too long. His mouth was much too big. And he had orange hair.

That is how he came to be called Prince Carrots.

The queen was very upset about the way he looked. It was not that his face was too wide. It was not that his nose was too long. It was not that his mouth was much too big. It was not even the color of his hair. It was the combination of those things. He was very hard to look at.

The queen's best friend was Mercury the Magician. Mercury knew she was upset about the way Prince Carrots looked.

"You must not worry," he said. "The prince will be very intelligent. People will love him because he is smart."

"Can you make him more handsome?" she asked.

"No," he said. "I cannot make him what he is not."

"Is there nothing you can do?" she asked.

"I can give him a special gift," he said. "He can give his intelligence to the person he loves the most."

The queen felt better. She tried not to look away from her son.

But every year, it was worse. The prince's face grew wider. His nose grew longer. His mouth grew bigger. His hair even seemed to become a brighter orange. It was even more orange than a carrot.

But he was very intelligent. He knew military strategies. He knew about all kinds of animals. He even knew some magic tricks. Everyone asked him questions. He always had the answers.

His father, the king, asked him questions.

"Do you know about the Trojan War?" the king asked.

"Of course, Father," Prince Carrots said. "Helen was kidnapped from Greece by a Trojan named Paris. Greek soldiers hid in a giant wooden horse. The horse was taken to the gates of Troy. The soldiers spilled out of the horse and attacked Troy. They wanted to rescue Helen because they loved her. She was very beautiful."

His mother, the queen, asked him questions, too.

"Where do the pearls on my necklace come from?" the queen asked.

"From an oyster," Prince Carrots said. "An oyster lives in the sea. When sand gets in its shell, it feels uncomfortable. It makes a pearl from the sand. Then the oyster feels better. Even sand can become beautiful."

Mercury the Magician also asked him questions.

"How do you make a strawberry disappear?" Mercury asked.

"Eat it as fast as you can," the prince said.

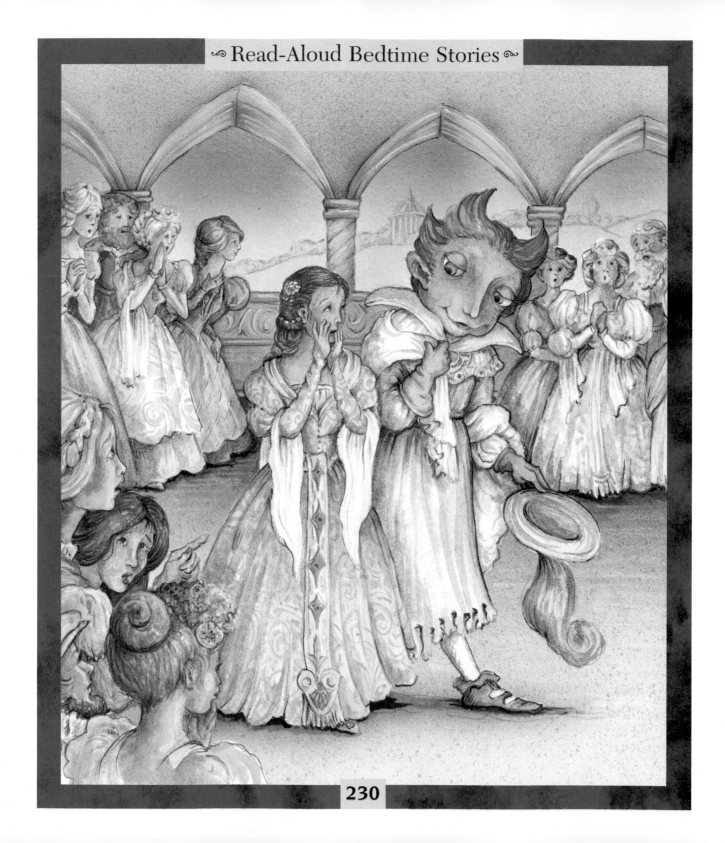

Prince Carrots also knew how to make people laugh. He knew the very best jokes. At parties, everyone gathered around him.

"Carrots are good for your eyes," he said.

"All carrots except Prince Carrots," someone said.

Everyone tried not to laugh at that. It was not nice to make fun of the prince. But when the prince smiled, they did, too.

"Very funny," he said. "But it is true."

"How do you know?" someone else asked.

"Have you ever seen a rabbit with glasses?" the prince asked.

Everyone laughed. The prince kept smiling. His mouth was much too big, but he had a nice smile.

A princess from a nearby kingdom noticed his smile. It was big, after all. She could not help it.

Prince Carrots saw the princess looking at him. He was surprised. He was surprised because she was the most beautiful princess he had ever seen.

She had a lovely face. Her nose was perfect. Her mouth was perfect. Her hair was perfect. He could not look away.

He went to her and introduced himself.

"I am Prince Carrots," he said.

The princess looked up at him, but she did not smile. The prince could not blame her. He knew he was hard to look at.

"I am Prince Carrots," he said again.

"I am Princess Pia," she said.

"I am honored to meet you," he said.

"It is I who am honored to meet you," she said.

"Really?" he asked. "You are?"

He was shocked. Princesses liked to meet him and ask questions. No princess was ever honored to meet him.

"Yes," she said. "You are very smart. I have been told that you are smart. I have been told more than a thousand times."

Still, she did not smile. The prince knew there was a reason. His face made people look away. It did not make them sad. The princess was sad.

He sat down next to her. He told her a joke, but she did not laugh. She just looked at him. Her eyes were blank. She did not understand his joke.

"Why are you so unhappy?" he asked her.

"I am not sure why," she said. "I only know that I am stupid."

"But you are very beautiful," he said.

"Yes," she said. "I have heard that a thousand times, too."

"How did you get to be so beautiful?" he asked.

"I was born that way," she said.

She told him a story. She had heard the story a thousand times. She only remembered things if she heard them a thousand times.

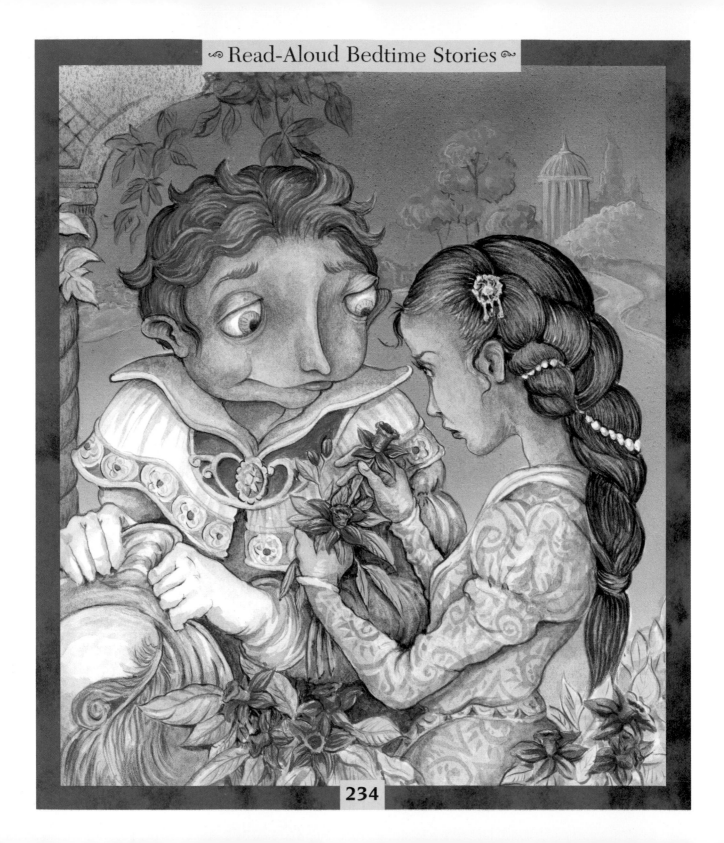

"My mother has a friend," the princess said. "He is a magician."

"Oh!" the prince said. "Mercury?"

"I think so. Yes!" the princess said.

The princess was quiet for a moment. Then her face went blank.

"You were talking about Mercury the Magician," the prince said.

"Oh, yes," she said. "The magician is my mother's friend. When I was young, she told him she was worried. She was worried about me. I was beautiful, but I was not very smart."

"You are very beautiful," the prince said.

He could not look away.

"But not very smart," the princess said. "My mother wanted him to make me more intelligent. He told her he could not. He could not make me something that I was not. That worried her. He told her not to worry. He told her I would be loved for my beauty."

The prince nodded when he heard that. The princess had to look away. He was so hard to look at.

"What happened after that?" the prince asked.

"Oh, well, my mother was still worried," she said. "The magician patted her hand. He told her he would give me a gift. He said I would be able to give my beauty to someone. I could give it to the person I loved the most."

The prince nodded again. Mercury had given him a similar gift.

Prince Carrots and Princess Pia spent the rest of the day together.

Prince Carrots heard the story about Mercury the Magician many times. The princess could not remember that she had already told him. He did not mind. He was happy to look upon her face and listen.

The princess found the prince to be a good listener. But he was hard to look at. When she looked away, he did not seem to mind. He smiled a lot. She liked that. It made her happy.

They enjoyed one another's company. They soon began to spend a lot of time together.

The prince loved to look at the princess. He also loved the way he felt around her. She did not ask a lot of questions. She did not expect him to tell jokes. He could relax with her. He could be himself. He did not even feel ugly when he was with her.

The princess loved the way she felt around the prince. He could not take his eyes from her. She did not mind. He liked to hear her talk. She knew she told him the same stories again and again. He never rolled his eyes. He did not tell her he had already heard them. She could relax with him. She could be herself. She did not even feel stupid when she was with him.

"You are very dear to me," the prince said.

The prince smiled at the princess. She smiled back at him.

"You are very dear to me, too," the princess said.

Prince Carrots fell in love with Princess Pia.

He did not tell her. He could not tell her. He did not want to lose her special friendship. She was much too dear to him. Besides, she was too beautiful to want to marry him. He was much too ugly.

Princess Pia fell in love with Prince Carrots.

She did not tell him. She could not tell him. She did not want to lose his special friendship. He was much too dear to her. Besides, he was too intelligent to want to marry her. She was much too stupid.

They still spent all their time together.

But things were different. Things were strange. They hardly knew how to act around each other.

"Did I ever tell you about the Trojan War?" he asked.

"Oh, yes," the princess said. "The Greeks rescued Helen because she was so beautiful."

Of course he had told her about the Trojan War! The funny thing was, he could not remember it.

"Did I tell you what happened at breakfast?" the princess asked.

"No," the prince said. "What happened at breakfast?"

"I told everyone about the Trojan War," she said.

The prince laughed! She had made him laugh. He looked wonderful when he laughed. She did not turn away.

When they were apart, Prince Carrots missed Princess Pia. He could not wait to see her. When he combed his hair carefully, he thought only of her. He was worried, though. He told the princess the same things over and over.

He was sure she thought he was stupid.

Princess Pia could not wait to see the prince. She always hurried to be with him. She did not want to forget things that happened at breakfast. She did not even bother to comb her hair.

She was sure he thought she was ugly.

"She is lovely even when her hair is tangled," the prince thought.

"He is smart to repeat things so I will remember," the princess thought.

"Will you marry me?" the prince asked.

He could not help himself. She was so beautiful.

"Yes!" the princess said.

She could not help herself. He was so smart.

Everyone was shocked when they heard the news.

"Why would she marry him? He is so hard to look at," some said.

"Why would he marry her? She is so stupid," others said.

No one could believe it. No one, that is, except Mercury the Magician. He knew love was like that.

It seems we become most what we want to be when we are in love. But what really happens is we are loved for what we truly are.

The Little Dutch Boy

Adapted by Brian Conway ▪ Illustrated by Linda Dockey Graves

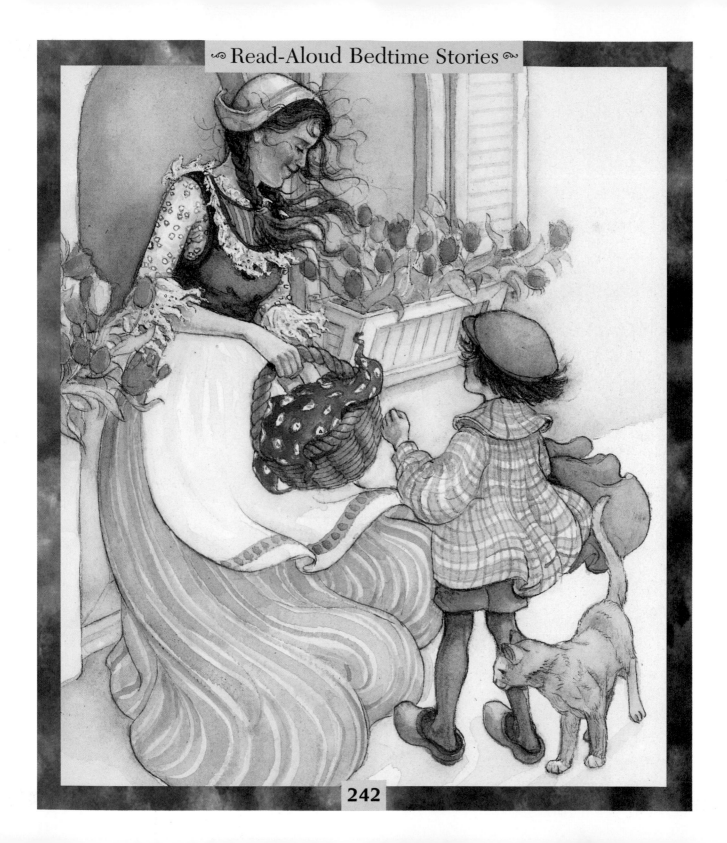

Once there was a little Dutch boy named Hans. He lived with his mother in a little town in Holland.

Holland is a very flat country. The town Hans lived in was by the sea. The farmers who lived there built big walls around their farms. The big walls, called dikes, kept the sea from flooding the farms.

Hans was a regular boy. He went to school with the other children in town. He played with his friends after school. He did his chores. He helped his mother whenever he could.

"Hans," his mother said. "I need you to take this basket of food to Mr. Van Notten."

Mr. Van Notten was an old friend of theirs. He lived on a farm on the edge of town. It was a long way to his house. The walk there and back always took most of the day.

"I wanted to go swimming," Hans said.

"You can swim tomorrow," his mother said. "Mr. Van Notten is waiting for you. Now, Mr. Van Notten always asks you to stay for dinner. What will you tell him?"

"I will thank him," Hans said. "But I will tell him I have to get home. It is a long walk."

"You are a good boy, Hans," his mother said. "I will have dinner waiting for you when you return."

Hans set off on the main road out of town. The dike was built alongside of the road. He tapped the dike with a stick as he walked. He thought about his friends. They were swimming at the beach.

He thought of Mr. Van Notten. Mr. Van Notten was an old man. He lived alone. He had only his old dog to keep him company. He was always very happy to have visitors.

"My dear friend!" Mr. Van Notten said. "I am so glad to see you!"

Hans smiled and shook Mr. Van Notten's hand. He gave Mr. Van Notten the big basket of food.

"Look at all of these wonderful things," Mr. Van Notten said. "Come inside. We will have a bite to eat."

Hans knew he had to start for home. But he was very thirsty after his long walk. Mr. Van Notten had hot cocoa warming on the fire.

"I can only stay for a cup of cocoa," he said.

Hans stayed for a cup of cocoa. He also stayed for a few stories. Mr. Van Notten told the best stories.

Hans lost track of time. He looked out the window. It was already beginning to get dark outside.

"Oh, no! It's getting dark," he said. "I must be getting home."

"It looks like a storm is coming," Mr. Van Notten said. "Hurry home. Be very careful if it starts to rain."

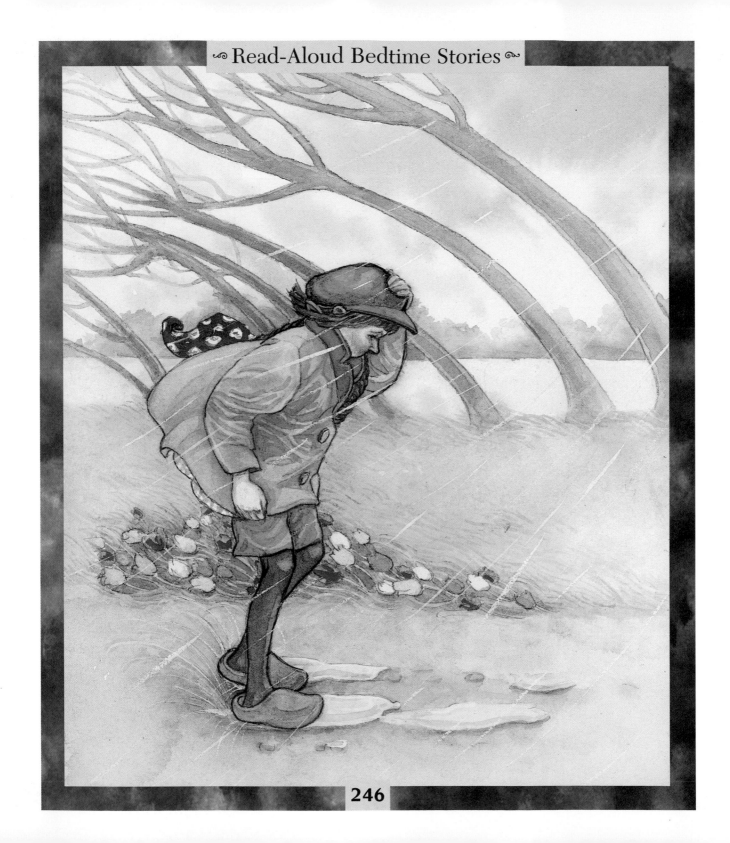

Hans walked up the road. He felt a few cold raindrops fall. The wind began to blow. The sky became very dark and stormy.

Hans pulled his hat down over his ears. The raindrops turned into sheets of rain. Every gust of cold wind made him walk faster. The storm got worse with every step.

The strong wind made the trees bend low. It blew the cold rain into his eyes. He walked into the wind. He slipped and slid along the muddy road. He could not walk very fast.

The wind knocked him back. It spun him around.

The rain was really bad. He could hardly see a thing in front of him.

"I hope this is the right direction," he said to himself.

He looked down at the mud at his feet.

"I hope I am still walking on the road," he thought.

Hans came around a corner in the road. The winds let up a little. He lifted his head and saw the dike in front of him.

"Thank goodness," he said. "I am almost home."

He went over to the dike. He would use it to lead him back home.

But something about the dike was not right. It was raining hard, but there was even more water. Seawater gushed from the stones. There was a crack in the wall.

The dike had sprung a leak!

Hans ran toward town. He felt his way along the dike through the storm. He hurried as fast as he could go.

"I must get to town and warn the others," he thought.

Hans never thought the dike could break. It was the strongest thing he knew. It was older than any building in town.

The dike had stood up to many fierce storms. Strong winds and crashing waves had never harmed it. The dike kept the little town safe.

But Hans had never seen a storm like this one before. The old stone wall was no match. The winds and waves were stronger. If the dike broke, the town would be washed away by the sea.

Hans arrived in town at last. The streets were dark and empty.

"The dike is leaking!" he shouted.

There was terrible thunder and howling winds.

"We must fix the dike!" he shouted.

No one could hear him.

"We are in danger!" he shouted.

His voice was nothing more than a squeak. The storm was too loud.

Hans did not see anyone. Every house was closed up. Every door was bolted shut. Every window was sealed and shuttered.

"Somebody help!" Hans shouted.

Nobody heard him.

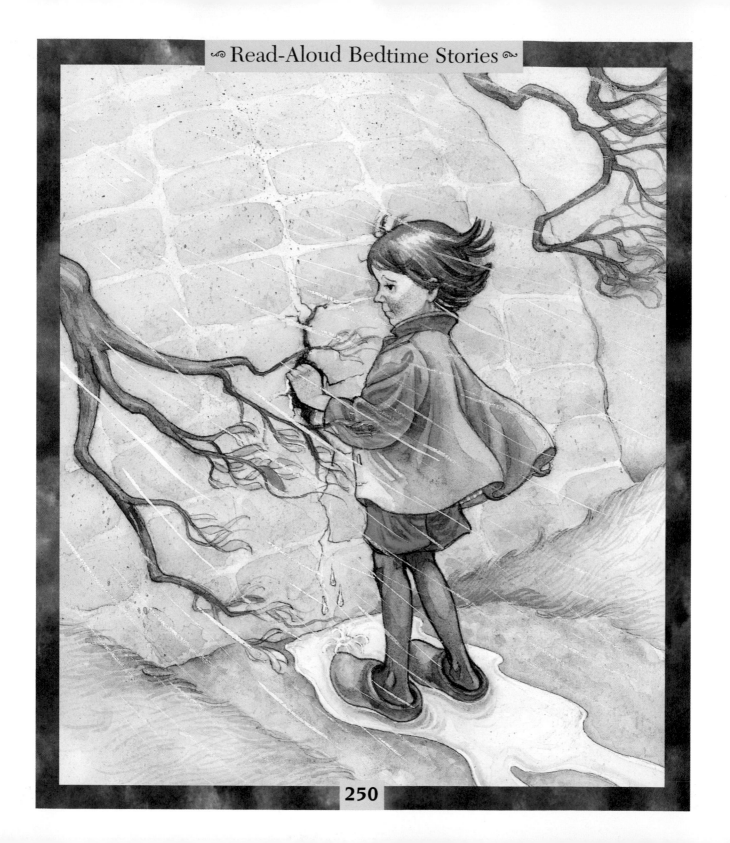

Hans thought of the dike. He thought of the crack in the stones. He was the only person who knew the town was in danger.

"There is no one to help me," he thought. "I will have to think of something. I will have to fix the dike."

Hans knew nothing about mending walls. He had no tools and no supplies. He ran back to the crack in the dike anyway.

The crack had grown bigger!

He looked around for something to cover the crack.

He found some branches. He put them into the crack. The seawater squirted around them.

He dug up a handful of mud. He put it into the crack. The seawater washed it away.

Hans was scared. He could hear waves pounding against the stone wall. The crack in the dike became a little bigger with every crash. The storm was not settling down. It was getting worse.

"I have to do something," he thought.

There was nothing left to plug the hole. Hans balled up his fist. He pushed it into the hole. The steady stream of cold water around it slowed down. The wall only dripped.

He had plugged up the hole. He was glad he had thought of something. But he was worried too. How long could he hold back the sea?

He tried not to think about that. He tried to be proud of his cleverness. He tried to feel strong as he held back the sea.

He knew his mother was worrying about him. He hoped she would send someone to look for him.

Moments became hours. The rain and winds became colder. No one came looking for him.

"No one will venture out in this storm," Hans thought.

He was still very scared. He was also very tired.

He was soaked through. His legs were shaking in the same muddy puddle. His arm ached as he continued to push it into the wall. His hand was frozen. He could hardly feel it.

"I must save the town," he said over and over again. "I must save the town. I must save the town."

Hans's mother was very worried. She had been waiting for Hans for a very long time. It was the middle of the night.

She opened her shutter to look out the window. The shutter snapped back. Wind and rain blew in.

"Oh, Hans," she said, "Where are you?"

She closed the window. She hoped that Hans had kept out of the storm. She hoped he had stayed in the safety of Mr. Van Notten's house. No one could survive outside during such a storm.

The storm settled down the next morning. Hans did not notice when the sun came up. He shivered with cold. His legs were exhausted.

He could no longer feel his hand. He had not let it drop from the wall. He still held back the rough morning tide.

Mr. Van Notten had worried all night about Hans. He wondered if Hans had made it home. He wanted to be sure. He called for his old dog. They walked toward town.

Mr. Van Notten walked toward the dike. He squinted and saw a familiar shape. When he got closer, he saw that it was Hans. His dear friend was holding back the sea with his little hand.

Hans sniffled and yawned. He shivered and shook. He did not hear Mr. Van Notten calling to him.

"My dear friend!" Mr. Van Notten said. " You are a hero. You've saved the town from a flood."

Hans looked up with a small smile.

"I must save the town," he said.

"You have saved the town," Mr. Van Notten said. "Hold on just a little while longer."

Mr. Van Notten hurried up the road to get help. The townspeople were just waking up. A group of people soon arrived at the dike. They brought tools and supplies to repair the dike. They brought dry blankets for Hans.

They carried him home to his mother. She was very happy to see him. She warmed his face with kisses. She held his worn fingers and rubbed his stiff legs. She fed him hot soup.

The doctor arrived to check on Hans. Hans was tucked into his warm, dry bed. He had the sniffles, but he was okay.

He was not scared anymore. He was safe.

"My brave little boy," his mother said. "You saved us all."

"I don't think I will go swimming today after all," Hans said.

Everyone heard about what Hans had done. They were proud of him.

"That one little boy saved our whole town," said the shoemaker.

"He held back the sea with just one hand," said the baker.

The mayor called all the townspeople together.

"Hans worked through the night to hold back the flood," he said. "He saved us all while we were asleep. While he is sleeping, we must prepare a celebration for him."

Hans woke up to the sound of a band playing. He peeked out his bedroom window. He saw every face in town in the street below. All the faces looked up at him and cheered.

The mayor presented Hans with a medal of honor. The little Dutch boy was a hero. Even after Hans was all grown up, everyone still called him the boy who saved the town.

Ali Baba

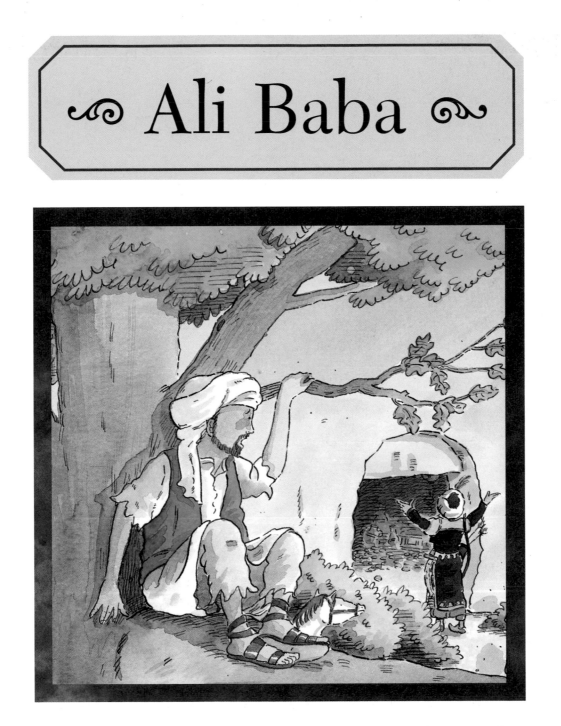

Adapted by Jennifer Boudart ▪ Illustrated by Anthony Lewis

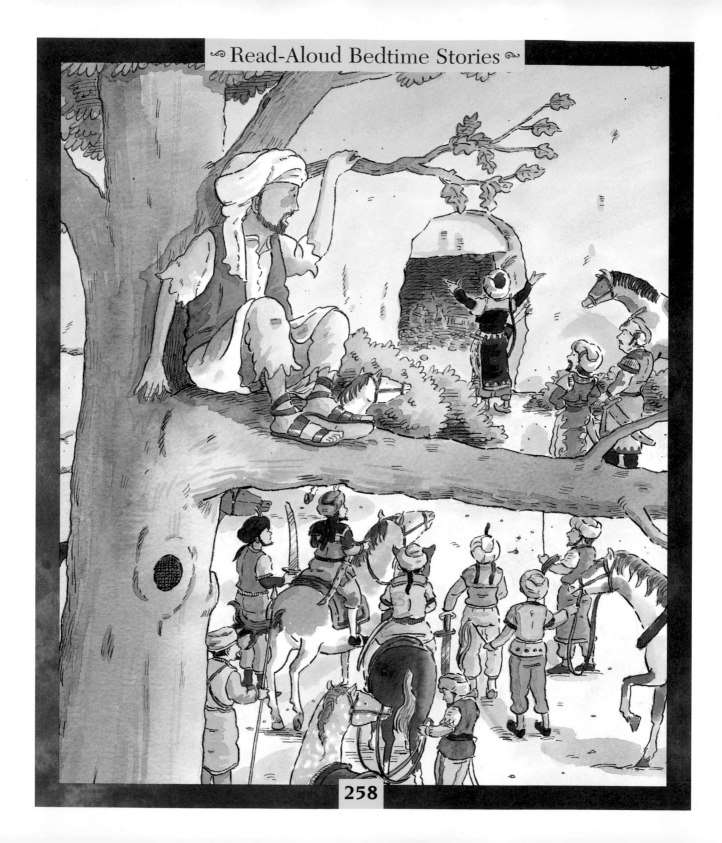

*I*n ancient times, there was a man named Ali Baba. He lived in Persia. He was a woodcutter. He had always been a woodcutter. He thought he would always be a woodcutter. But that changed one day.

One day, Ali Baba was working in the forest. He climbed a tree to cut a high branch. He stopped chopping when he heard the sound of hoofbeats. A group of riders came. They did not look like friendly men to Ali Baba. They looked like thieves.

They rode beneath his tree. He counted them as they passed. There were forty riders. The number made him think. A band of forty thieves traveled around Persia. They stole anything and everything. They did not mind hurting people to do it.

The men stopped their horses near a rock wall. Each rider pulled a heavy bag from his saddle.

"Open sesame!" the leader said.

A door opened in the rocks.

Ali Baba watched the men go inside. When they came back, they did not have the bags. They had left the bags inside.

The captain came out last.

"Close sesame!" he said.

The rock door shut tight.

Ali Baba watched the men ride away. He knew it was the famous band of thieves. No one knew where the band had its hideout. He had just found it. He climbed down and stood before the wall.

"Open sesame!" he said.

The door opened.

Ali Baba put down his ax and went inside.

There was not much light in the cave. He took a step inside. He squinted his eyes to see better. The floor was covered with coins!

He began to search the cave. It was filled with riches. There were colorful rugs, silver bowls, gold bars, and shiny jewels. He also found the bags of coins the thieves had brought. He grabbed all the bags he could carry.

"Close sesame!" he said.

The door shut tight.

Ali Baba raced home in his wagon. When his wife saw the coins, she was shocked. She was also scared.

"Did you break the law or hurt anyone?" she asked.

"No. This money came from the thieves," he said. "They have hurt many people. We must use it for good."

He told her about the thieves and their hideout. He told her about all the things they had left behind. He did not realize he had left something behind, too. He left his ax on the ground outside the cave.

Ali Baba used the money for good. He moved his family into a better house. He opened a shop. The shop was filled with fine goods at fair prices. It was soon a busy place.

The forty thieves were busy, too. It was a long time before they returned to their hideout.

"Open sesame!" the captain said.

The door opened. When it did, something on the ground caught his eye. It was an ax. The ax did not belong to any of his men. They carried knives. They had not stolen it. It was worthless. The thieves ran into the cave. They had been robbed!

The captain went to the smartest man in his band.

"Go to town," he said. "Find a poor man who is newly rich. Get his name. We will get even with him!"

The man went to town. He dressed like a trader. The first shop he visited belonged to Ali Baba. Morgiana was working for Ali Baba that day. She was a good worker and a good friend.

"I am a trader," the man said. "I have never seen this shop before."

"It is new," she said. "It belongs to Ali Baba."

"Interesting," the man said.

"He is not trading right now though," she said.

Morgiana did not like the way the trader looked.

"Too bad," the man said. "Does Ali Baba own any other shops?"

"This is the only one," she said. "He just got the money to open it."

The trader thanked Morgiana and smiled. She did not like that smile.

The man went back to his captain.

"I have a name. It's Ali Baba," he said. "He just got some money. He opened a shop. He lives the life of a rich man."

The captain gave the thief a piece of white chalk.

"Return to Ali Baba's shop. Mark an **X** on the door so we will know it. We will break into the shop and teach Ali Baba a lesson," the captain said.

When it was dark, the thief returned to town. He went to the shop. The street was almost empty. Only one woman was walking there. The thief smiled to himself.

He did not know the woman was watching him. It was Morgiana. She had seen him smile. She remembered that smile. It belonged to the tricky trader.

The thief marked an **X** on Ali Baba's shop. He dropped the chalk and walked away.

Morgiana guessed the mark meant trouble for Ali Baba. She picked up the chalk. She marked an **X** on all the doors along the street.

The captain and his men arrived later that night. Every door along the street had a chalk mark. The thieves did not know which shop to strike. They were very angry. The captain was the angriest of all.

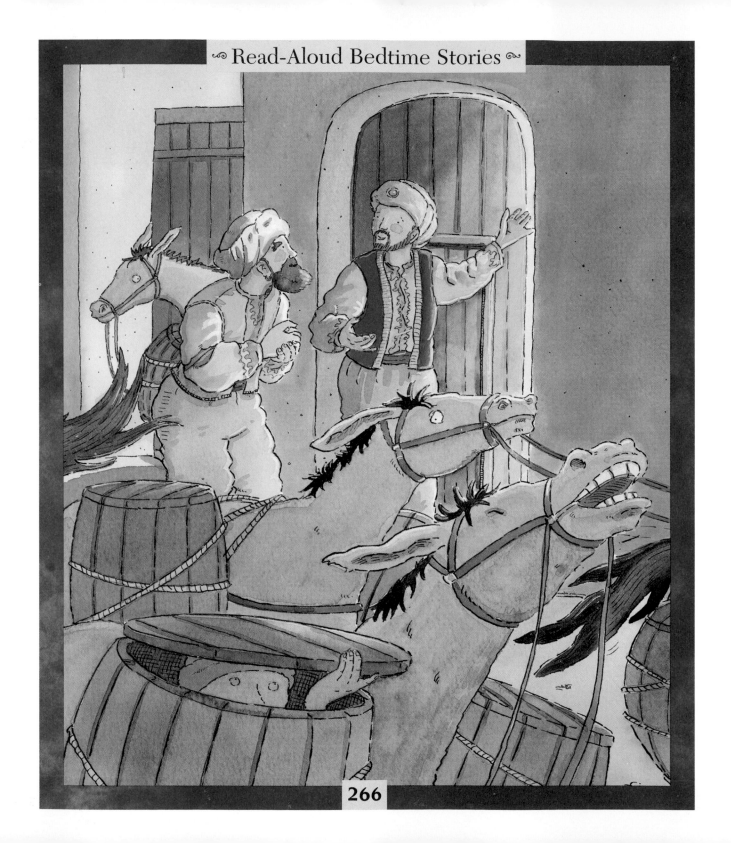

The forty thieves held a meeting the next day.

"Someone figured out our chalk trick," the angry captain said. "I have a plan that will not fail."

He told them his plan.

The thieves lined up twenty mules. Each mule carried two large oil barrels. All the barrels were empty. The men climbed into them.

The captain screwed the lids on the barrels. He covered his hair with a scarf. He put on a fake beard. He led the mules toward town.

Ali Baba heard a knock on the door of his shop. He opened it to find a man with twenty mules.

"Can I help you?" Ali Baba asked.

"I have come to town to sell my oil," the man said. "There is no room at the inn. I wondered if I might sleep in your stable."

"Your mules can stay in my stable," Ali Baba said. "But I ask that you stay at my house."

The man quickly agreed. Ali Baba took the man home with him.

"Dinner is almost ready," Ali Baba said.

The man took the mules to the stable. He gave each one hay and water. He whispered into each barrel.

"Stay here until you hear my whistle. Then we will attack," he said.

He left the stable and went to the house.

The man was not Ali Baba's only guest. Morgiana was also staying with Ali Baba and his family.

When everyone went to bed, Morgiana could not sleep. She went to the kitchen for some tea. She needed oil to heat the water. There was none left. She thought of the other guest and all his oil. She did not think he would mind if she took some.

She walked to the stable. She turned the lid on one of the barrels. Inside the barrel, a voice whispered.

"Is it time?" the voice asked.

"No, not yet," she whispered back.

Morgiana tested all forty barrels. Whispers came from all but one. Why would men hide in oil barrels? She did not know. She just knew it meant trouble for Ali Baba.

She had to think quickly. She rolled up some hay and set it on fire. She opened the lid of one barrel.

"Go quietly or this fire goes in with you," she said.

The man jumped out and ran. She went to every barrel and said the same thing. She scared all the men away.

The captain came out. He whistled. All was quiet. He checked the barrels. He found that they were empty. He knew he had been found out.

He ran, too.

Ali Baba thanked Morgiana for being so brave. He wanted to reward her. He made her a partner at the shop. He also hired guards for protection.

The captain watched Ali Baba and his guards. He could not believe his plan had failed. He was angry. He was so angry he sent all his men away. He would deal with Ali Baba himself.

The captain shaved his head. He took a new name. He became Hassan. He opened a shop next to Ali Baba's shop. Hassan and Ali Baba became friends. Ali Baba had no idea who Hassan really was.

"Will you come for dinner?" Ali Baba asked.

"Nothing would make me happier," Hassan said.

Morgiana also came to dinner. She noticed Hassan was wearing a very beautiful robe. She also noticed he kept reaching beneath it. She saw a flash of silver. He was hiding a knife!

Morgiana knew this man. He was the lying oil merchant. She had to do something to protect Ali Baba.

"Ali Baba," she said, "I must dance for your friend."

She danced with scarves. She circled the chair where Hassan sat. She tied him up tightly with the scarves.

Morgiana pulled the knife out from Hassan's robe.

"This man wants to hurt you, Ali Baba," she said. "He is none other than the lying oil merchant."

Ali Baba's guards took Hassan to jail. They came back with big news. Hassan was a famous thief. He was the captain of the forty thieves.

Everything became clear to Ali Baba. The captain knew he had robbed the hideout. He wanted to hurt Ali Baba and his family in return. The captain had failed because Morgiana was so smart.

"Morgiana, you saved my family," Ali Baba said.

"You would have done the same for me," she said.

The police chief visited Ali Baba's house. Many towns had been robbed by the forty thieves.

"Each town offered money to anyone who caught them," the chief said. "You have done so. All that money is yours."

He gave Ali Baba a heavy bag. It was filled with coins. Ali Baba knew just what to do with it.

He gave it to Morgiana.

"I want you to have this money," he said.

"I cannot take it," she said. "This money would make your life perfect. You could even open another shop."

"My life is already perfect," he said. "Money cannot buy good friends like you. Take it and open your own shop."

Morgiana did. She opened a shop next to Ali Baba's shop. She worked hard. She was a good friend. She was very happy.

Paradise

Adapted by Lisa Harkrader ■ Illustrated by Amy Flynn

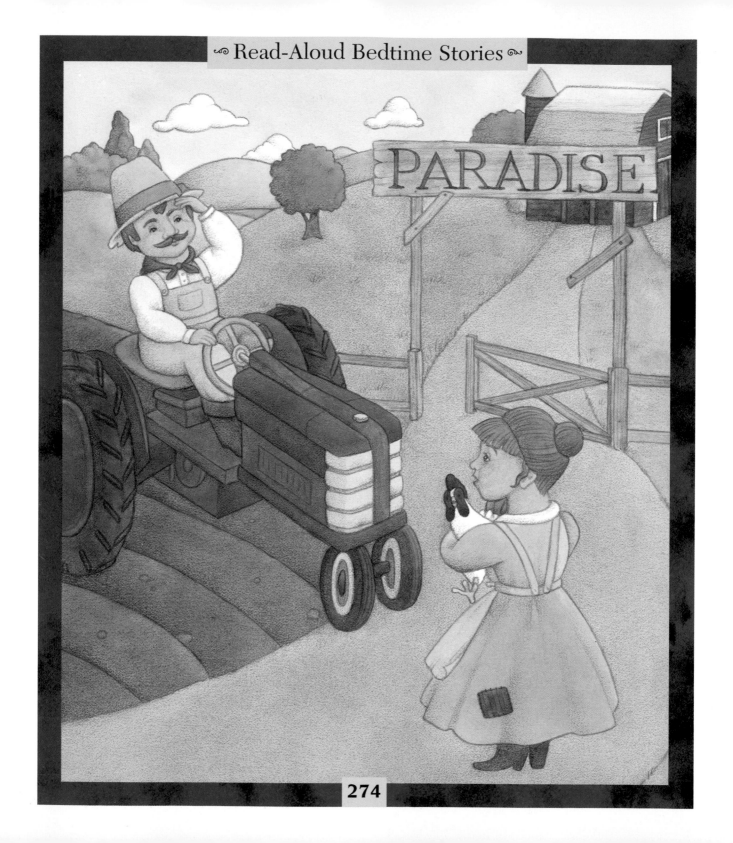

om and Lucy were married. They lived on a farm, but they did not have much. They had an old plow. They had an old tractor. They had an old hen named Madge.

The name of their farm was Paradise.

"But it doesn't feel like paradise," Tom always said.

Tom and Lucy worked very hard, but they were very poor. Tom was really busy. He could not plow, plant, and pick the corn by himself.

Lucy tried to plow, but the plow got stuck. She tried to plant, but most of the seed blew away. She tried to pick the corn, but she pulled too hard. All the corn was ruined.

More corn needed to be planted. But they had no more money to buy more seed.

"We'll have to sell Madge," Tom said.

"Brawk," Madge said.

"I'll take her to the bird farm down the road," Tom said.

"Brawk," Madge said.

"While you are gone," Lucy said, "I'll plow the field."

"Brawk, brawk, brawk," Madge said.

"No," Tom said. "I'd better plow the field myself. You can take Madge to the bird farm."

Lucy set off down the road with Madge under her arm.

Lucy walked and walked. Madge cackled and squawked. They reached the bird farm.

"BRAWWWK!" Madge said.

She fluttered from Lucy's arms and flapped across the barnyard. Lucy ran after her.

Madge flapped through a puddle.

Lucy fell in the puddle. Mud splashed all over her.

Madge flapped through the goose pen.

Lucy slid through the goose pen. Geese honked at her.

Madge flapped through the duck pen.

Lucy skidded through the duck pen. Ducks quacked at her.

Madge flapped through the turkey pen. She fluttered through the chicken pen. She flew through the peacock pen.

Lucy tripped on a turkey. She flipped over a chicken. She landed beside a peacock.

Mud and eggs and feathers landed on top of her. Geese and ducks honked and quacked. Turkeys and chickens gobbled and clucked. The peacock shrieked.

Madge flapped and flapped. She flapped out of the barnyard. She flapped down the road toward Paradise.

Lucy picked herself up and ran after her.

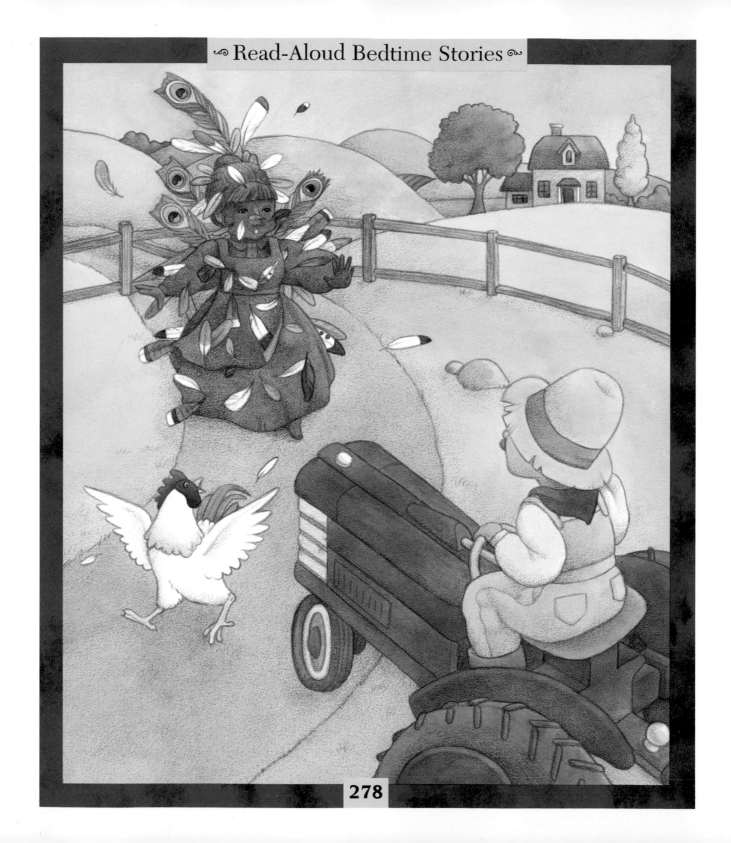

"BRAWWWK!"

Tom heard Madge squawk. He looked up.

Madge ran down the road as fast as she could. Something strange ran after Madge as fast as it could.

Tom stared at them.

The strange creature was as big as a person. It had goose feathers on its head. It had duck feathers on its arms. It had turkey feathers on its belly. It had chicken feathers on its back.

Trailing behind it were the lovely tail feathers of a peacock.

They ran down the road. They leaped over the fence.

The strange creature ran toward Tom. It looked up at him on the tractor. It opened its mouth to speak.

"I didn't sell Madge," it said. "I didn't get the corn seed. But look at all the lovely feathers I brought back."

Tom stared at the strange creature.

"Lucy? Is that you?" he asked.

Lucy nodded.

"We had a little accident at the bird farm," she said. "I don't think Madge wants to be sold."

"Well, I'll sell her," Tom said.

He set off down the road with Madge under his arm.

Tom walked and walked. Madge cackled and squawked. They came upon a house.

A woman was standing in the yard. She held a cup in one hand. She raised the cup over her head. She counted to ten.

"Full!" she said.

She slapped her hand over the top of the cup. She ran inside the house.

"Oh, no!" Tom heard the woman cry. "Not again!"

She came back outside with the cup. She looked upset. Tom decided to introduce himself.

"Howdy, ma'am," he said. "My name is Tom. I live down the road at a place called Paradise."

"Hello," the woman said.

"Do you need help?" Tom asked.

"Yes, I do," the woman said. "I'm trying to take the beautiful sunshine into my kitchen."

"In a cup?" Tom said.

"Yes," the woman said. "Sunshine flows into the cup when I stand outside. I put my hand over the cup so it won't escape. Then I run inside."

"But when you lift your hand," Tom said, "the sunshine is always gone."

"Yes," the woman said. "I would give one hundred dollars to bring sunshine into my house."

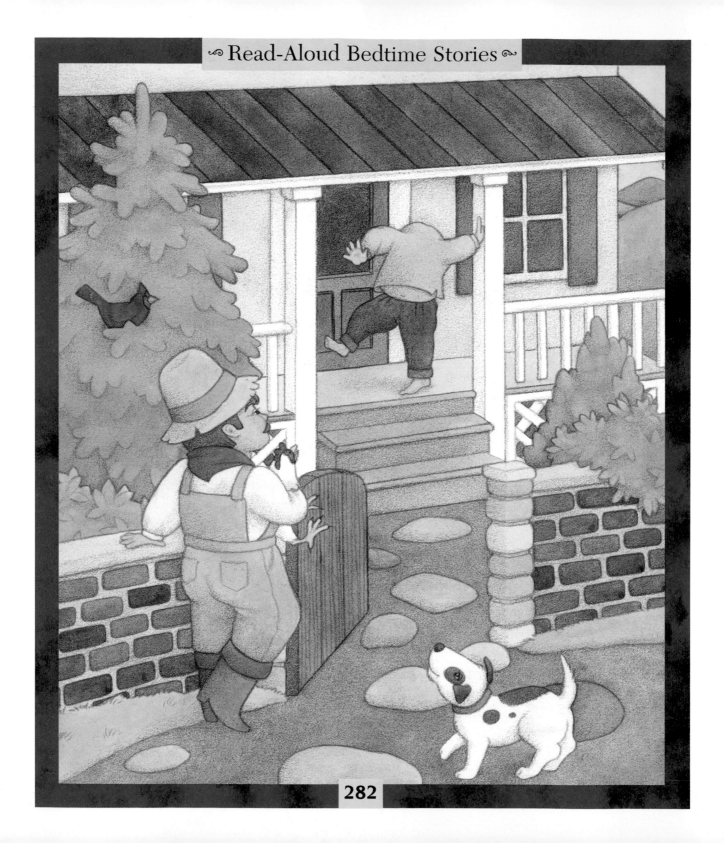

"You want sunshine inside your house?" Tom asked. "That's easy."

He picked up an ax. He chopped a hole in her wall.

"Now you have a window," he said.

"I wanted to make a window," the woman said. "I was afraid it would be too much work. Thank you!"

She handed Tom one hundred dollars.

Tom tried to give it back. The woman insisted.

"Take it," she said. "It will make me happy."

Tom put the money in his pocket. He set off down the road carrying Madge under his arm.

He walked and walked. Madge cackled and squawked.

They came upon another house. A man stood on the porch. He was struggling to put on a shirt. His arms were through the sleeves, but his head was stuck. There was no hole for his head.

"Howdy, sir," Tom said. "My name is Tom. I live down the road at a place called Paradise."

"Hello," the man said.

"Do you need help?" Tom asked.

"Yes, I do," the man said. "I want to wear this shirt."

"But you can't get it over your head," Tom said.

"No," the man said. "I would give two hundred dollars to wear this shirt."

"You want to wear this shirt?" Tom asked. "That's easy."

He asked the man for a pair of scissors. He snipped a hole in the top.

"Now you have a neck hole," he said.

"I wanted to make a neck hole," the man said. "I was afraid it would be too much work. Thank you!"

He handed Tom two hundred dollars.

Tom tried to give it back. The man insisted.

"Take it," he said. "It will make me happy."

Tom put the money in his pocket. He set off down the road carrying Madge under his arm.

Tom walked and walked. Madge cackled and squawked.

They came upon another house. A woman sat on the porch. She was crying into a handkerchief.

"Howdy, ma'am," Tom said. "My name is Tom. I live down the road at a place called Paradise."

"Hello," the woman said.

"Do you need help?" Tom asked.

"You're from paradise?" the woman asked.

"Yes, I am," Tom said.

"You are just the man I wanted to see," the woman said. "I'd give three hundred dollars for a new suit."

"A new suit?" Tom asked.

"For my husband," the woman said.

"That's easy. Go to town and buy one," Tom said.

"It's not that simple," the woman said. "My husband died. We buried him in his work clothes. I wanted to make him a new suit. I was afraid it would be too much work. I've been sorry ever since."

"Don't be sorry," Tom said. "I'm sure your husband understands. I'm sure he's happy."

"I don't want him wearing work clothes in paradise," the woman said. "You're from paradise. Could you give him this money to buy a new suit?"

She handed Tom three hundred dollars.

Tom tried to give it back. The woman insisted.

"Take it," she said. "It will make me happy."

Tom put the money in his pocket. He set off down the road carrying Madge under his arm.

"Those people were all alike," he said. "They were all silly. They were all crazy. They were all afraid of too much work. Now I've got six hundred dollars! That's more than enough for corn seed. It's enough to live on for years. I don't need to sell my chicken."

"Brawk," Madge said.

Tom turned around and headed back to Paradise.

Tom walked and walked. Madge did not cackle or squawk. She snuggled up under his arm and took a nap.

When they reached Paradise, Tom stopped and stared.

All the fields were plowed. All the fields were planted in feathers. Goose feathers. Duck feathers. Turkey feathers. Chicken feathers. Peacock feathers. They all swayed in the breeze.

Lucy saw Tom and Madge and leaped from the tractor. She ran to the road to greet Tom and Madge.

"I would have planted corn," Lucy said.

"But you didn't have any seed," Tom said.

"That's right. I only had feathers," Lucy said.

"You must have worked hard," Tom said.

"Yes, I did," Lucy said. "I'm not afraid of hard work. I think I did a good job. What do you think?"

"What do I think?" Tom asked.

A breeze blew across the farm. Goose feathers fluttered. Duck feathers fluttered. Turkey feathers fluttered. Chicken feathers fluttered. Peacock feathers fluttered.

Tom smiled. He had money in his pocket. He had a wife who worked hard. He even had his chicken.

"What do I think?" he asked. "I think our farm is paradise."

Rikki-Tikki-Tavi

Adapted by Brian Conway ▪ Illustrated by Richard Bernal

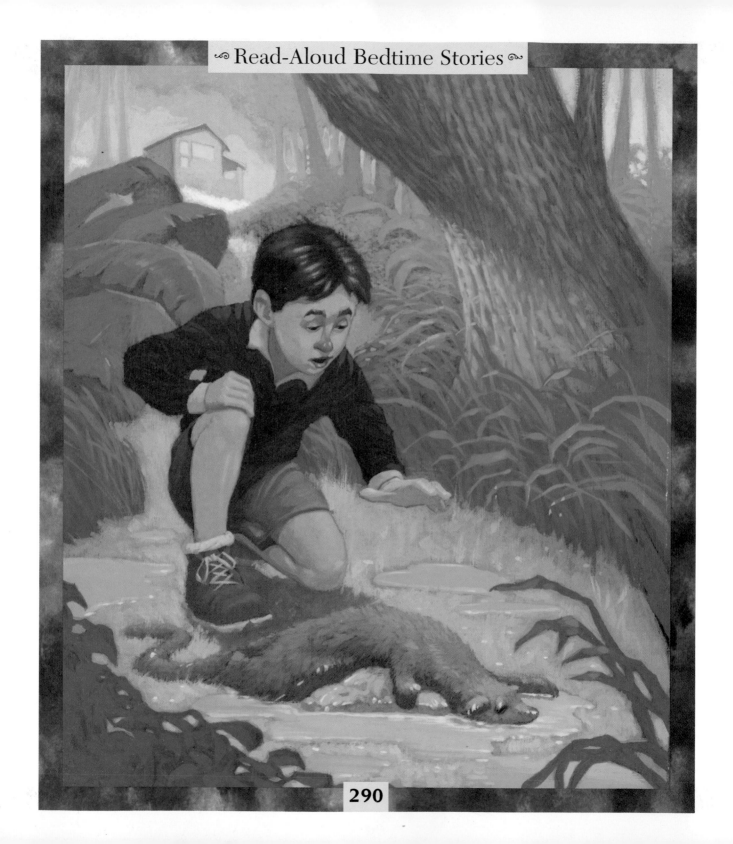

This is the story of a brave little mongoose. His name was Rikki-Tikki-Tavi. Every mongoose is little, fast, and furry. But not many mongooses were ever as brave as Rikki-Tikki-Tavi.

Rikki-Tikki-Tavi lived in India, a faraway country. He lived inside a hill in the jungle. A hole inside the hill was his home. One day, a big flood rushed through the jungle. It swept Rikki-Tikki-Tavi out of his hole. The rushing water carried him away.

Rikki-Tikki-Tavi bumped and rolled with the water. He thrashed his long, bushy tail. He was brave, but he could not fight the flood.

The flood was over in a flash. Rikki-Tikki-Tavi had been washed away. He was far from his home. His back hurt. His head hurt. Even the tip of his long tail hurt. He lay there in a puddle for a long time. He was very weak. He could barely move.

Rikki-Tikki-Tavi heard voices around him.

"Something died in the road," a boy said.

"Is it a cat, Teddy?" asked his mother.

"I think it's a rat," said Teddy.

Rikki-Tikki-Tavi lifted his head a bit.

"It's a mongoose," said Teddy's father.

"A mongoose?" asked Teddy. "I have never seen one before."

"It is still alive, but just barely," said Teddy's father.

The boy picked Rikki-Tikki-Tavi up from the mud. He wrapped him in his shirt and carried him home. His parents brought out a towel for him. Rikki-Tikki-Tavi was wet and cold. The soft, dry towel warmed him up.

"Rub the towel over his fur, Teddy," said the boy's mother. "The little guy is soaked through."

Rikki-Tikki-Tavi liked being under the towel. He felt safe there. The towel tickled his nose. He let out a sneeze. He shook the last few drops of muddy water from his fur. Teddy and his mother and father laughed.

Rikki-Tikki-Tavi started to feel better. He poked his head out from under the towel. He looked around. His new friends looked very kind.

Rikki-Tikki-Tavi brushed his little pink nose against Teddy's chin.

"Hey, that tickles," Teddy said.

"He wants to be your friend," said Teddy's father.

"Can I keep him?" Teddy asked.

"He is a wild animal," his mother said.

"You can't keep a wild animal," his father said. "He will go wherever he wants to go."

Rikki-Tikki-Tavi ducked back under the towel for a little nap.

"Well, it looks like this is where he wants to be," Teddy's father said.

Everyone laughed again. Rikki-Tikki-Tavi liked that. It made him feel much better.

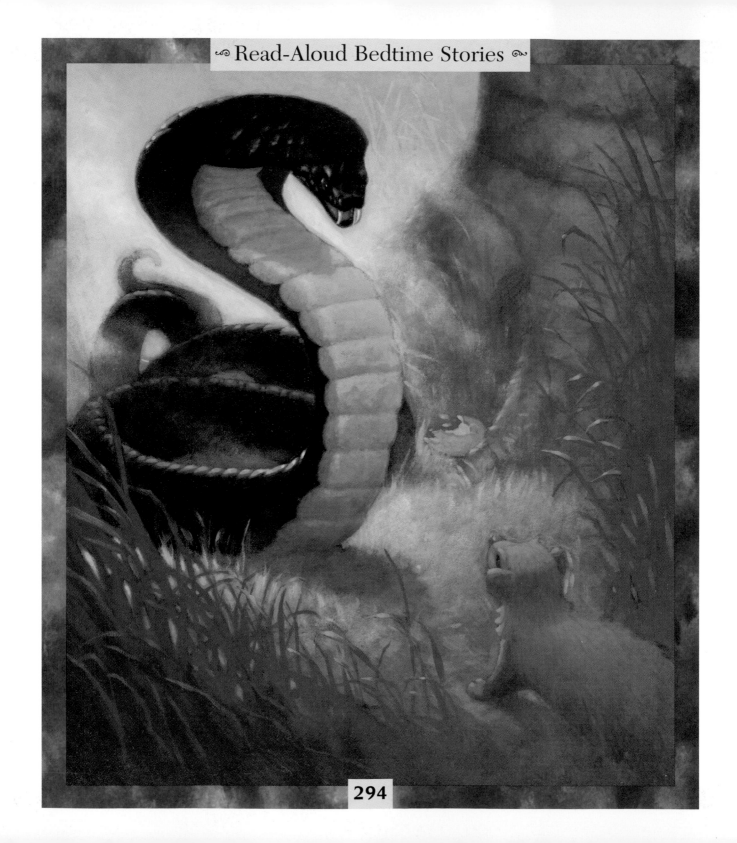

Rikki-Tikki-Tavi liked Teddy's house. It was warm and clean. Teddy was always willing to play with him. At bedtime, he crawled under the covers to sleep beside Teddy.

Rikki-Tikki-Tavi still wanted to do the things a wild mongoose did. He liked to play in the garden. He liked to run under the rosebushes and through the grass.

In the garden, Rikki-Tikki-Tavi made many new animal friends. His best friend was Darzee. She was a beautiful songbird.

"Am I the only mongoose around?" he asked Darzee.

"I have never seen anyone quite like you," Darzee said.

Rikki-Tikki-Tavi felt special. He was the only mongoose around. He liked the idea of being the only mongoose around. He ran back through the yard. The garden was his own little jungle kingdom.

Suddenly, Rikki-Tikki-Tavi heard Darzee shriek. He rushed to the tree where she lived.

"My egg!" she cried. "It fell from my nest, and Nag slithered off with it!"

"Who is Nag?" asked Rikki-Tikki-Tavi.

Rikki-Tikki-Tavi heard a low hiss behind him. He turned with a start. A big, deadly snake looked down on him.

"Who is Nag?" the snake hissed. "I am Nag!"

The snake had angry red eyes. It stared at Rikki-Tikki-Tavi.

"My family has ruled this garden for thousands of years," Nag said. "Every animal here must fear me."

Rikki-Tikki-Tavi was not afraid of Nag. Nag was a cobra. Cobras were one of the deadliest snakes in the world. But Rikki-Tikki-Tavi was a mongoose. A mongoose is one of the few animals unafraid of cobras.

"I do not fear you, Nag," Rikki-Tikki-Tavi said.

Rikki-Tikki-Tavi was ready to fight. His eyes turned a deep red just like Nag's eyes.

Nag had a surprise of his own. There were two snakes living in the garden. Nag had a wife. Her name was Nagaina. She appeared behind Rikki-Tikki-Tavi.

"Look out!" yelled Darzee.

Nagaina struck at Rikki-Tikki-Tavi with her fangs. Rikki-Tikki-Tavi hopped out of her way. The two snakes escaped by sliding away into the tall grass.

That night, Teddy and his parents slept. Rikki-Tikki-Tavi stayed awake. He peeked his head out from under Teddy's warm covers. He heard the sound of snakes moving along the rug. He also heard voices.

Rikki-Tikki-Tavi went toward the bathroom. The snakes were whispering in the dark. Rikki-Tikki-Tavi crept closer until he could hear what they were saying. He listened carefully.

Nag and Nagaina were making evil plans.

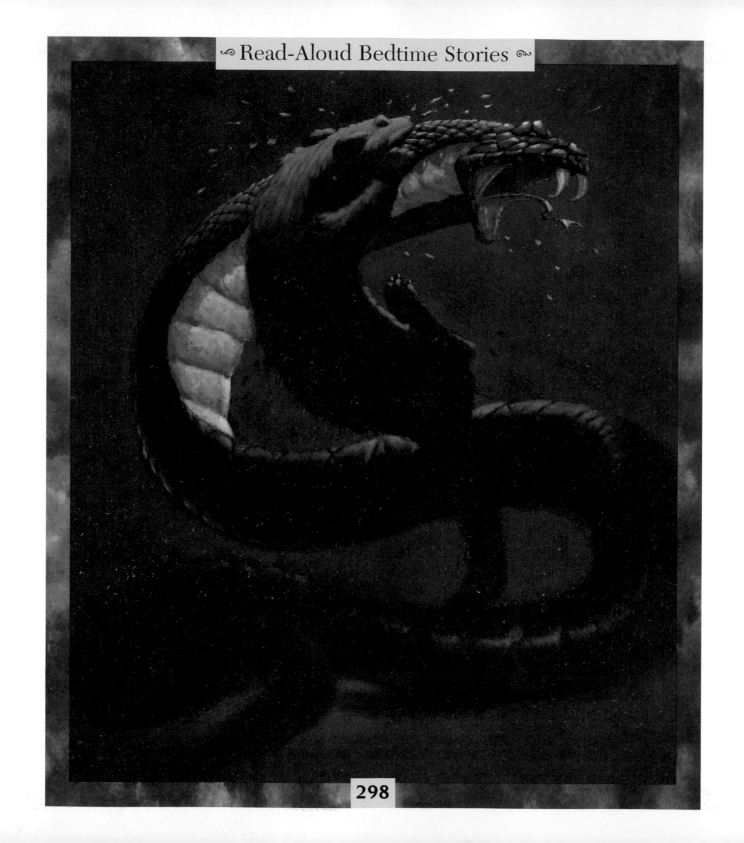

"We must scare the big ones away," Nag whispered. "The people will be gone. There will be no one to help the little mongoose."

"Then the garden will be ours again," Nagaina said. "Our eggs will hatch soon. We will raise our children to rule this place."

"We will rule for a thousand more years," Nag said.

Rikki-Tikki-Tavi's eyes glowed a deep red. He did not like the snakes in the house.

"Go into the bedroom," Nagaina told Nag. "I will wait outside. When the people come running out, I will be waiting."

"We will take care of the mongoose together," Nag said.

Nagaina slithered out to the yard. Nag slithered up the hall toward the bedrooms.

Rikki-Tikki-Tavi watched Nag move away. He had to be sure to be quiet. He crept up behind him. He used his quick little legs to leap up. He landed on the snake's neck.

Nag twisted and turned. He whipped his head around. Rikki-Tikki-Tavi held on to his neck. He did not want the cobra's fangs to reach him.

Rikki-Tikki-Tavi bit the snake. He would not let go. Nag hissed. Rikki-Tikki-Tavi held on. The snake could not shake him off.

Rikki-Tikki-Tavi heard a loud sound. He didn't know what happened, but Nag's body went limp.

Rikki-Tikki-Tavi saw Teddy's father standing over them. He had a broomstick. He had hit Nag over the head with it. He dropped it and picked up Rikki-Tikki-Tavi. The brave mongoose was not harmed.

"Teddy!" his mother called. "Your mongoose has just saved our lives!"

Rikki-Tikki-Tavi knew he would have to fight Nagaina. She would find out Nag was dead and want revenge. She would hurt Rikki-Tikki-Tavi's family.

Rikki-Tikki-Tavi made sure his family was safe. Then he went outside. He found Darzee in the garden. He told her how he had beaten Nag. He told her how he planned to send Nagaina away.

"I am going to find Nagaina's eggs," Rikki-Tikki-Tavi said. "You must help me by keeping Nagaina busy."

"I will keep her away for as long as I can," Darzee said.

Darzee hopped toward the house. Nagaina was crying near the porch.

"Oh, my," Darzee said. "My wing is broken. I cannot fly."

Nagaina heard Darzee's cries. She slithered toward the bird. Darzee hopped away from the house. She hopped away from the garden. Nagaina followed her. She did not know Darzee was pretending.

Rikki-Tikki-Tavi waited for Nagaina to leave the garden. Then he carried her eggs away. Darzee flew over him when he had the last egg.

"Hurry, Rikki-Tikki-Tavi!" she said. "Nagaina is on the porch! She has trapped Teddy and his family!"

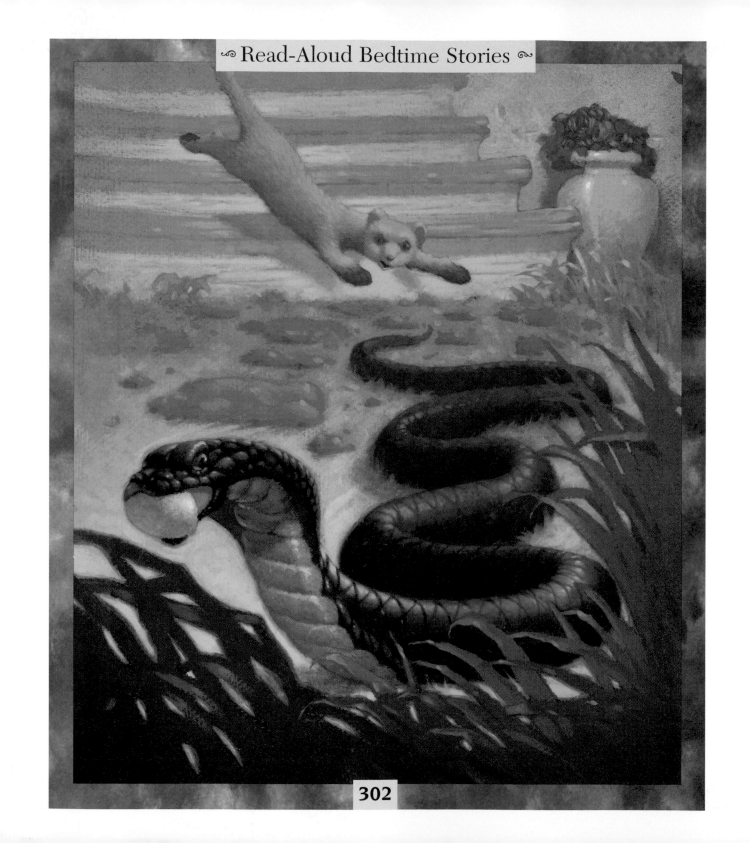

Rikki-Tikki-Tavi ran as fast as he could to the house.

Teddy's family stood in a corner of the porch. Nagaina faced them with her red eyes. She hissed and slithered closer to them. Teddy and his parents were very afraid. Their faces were very white.

Nagaina was ready to strike. She turned first toward Teddy.

Rikki-Tikki-Tavi rushed up the steps to the porch. He dropped the last egg beside Nagaina.

"I have the last of your eggs here," Rikki-Tikki-Tavi said. "The rest are now hidden from you."

Nagaina turned her angry eyes on Rikki-Tikki-Tavi.

"My babies! What have you done with them?" she hissed.

Rikki-Tikki-Tavi glared back at her. He had not been afraid of Nag. He was not afraid of Nagaina. He would not back down from her.

Teddy and his parents ran into the house. They looked through the window as the terrible fight began.

Nagaina snapped at Rikki-Tikki-Tavi. He leapt away from her deadly fangs. He was quick. He turned and dodged each of Nagaina's strikes. Nagaina twisted in her own angry dance. Her tail hit the egg. The egg rolled off the porch.

Before Rikki-Tikki-Tavi could stop her, Nagaina slid toward her egg. She snatched it up in her mouth and slithered away.

Nagaina hurried to bring her egg to safety. She rushed to her hole near the melon patch. Rikki-Tikki-Tavi followed her.

Darzee flew at the snake. Nagaina did not even slow down.

Rikki-Tikki-Tavi ran as fast as he could. He was close behind Nagaina. He could smell her fear.

Nagaina slid into her hole. Rikki-Tikki-Tavi leapt for her tail. He grabbed it and held on. Nagaina dragged him down into the hole.

The fight continued. Rikki-Tikki-Tavi bit and clawed at Nagaina. She dropped her egg, and Rikki-Tikki-Tavi grabbed her head. If she moved, she would crush her last egg.

"I will not harm you or your family," Rikki-Tikki-Tavi said. "But you must promise you will not harm my family."

"Where are my eggs?" Nagaina hissed.

"I put them in the meadow beside the river," Rikki-Tikki-Tavi answered boldly. "They are safe. Get them and never return here."

Nagaina agreed with a hiss. She took her egg and left the garden. She would not come back. She was gone forever.

Teddy and his parents had saved Rikki-Tikki-Tavi after the flood. Rikki-Tikki-Tavi had returned their kindness. He lived with them for a long time. His nights were spent under Teddy's warm covers. His days were spent playing in the garden. It was his own little jungle kingdom.

The Golden Goose

Adapted by Jennifer Boudart ■ Illustrated by Karen Dugan

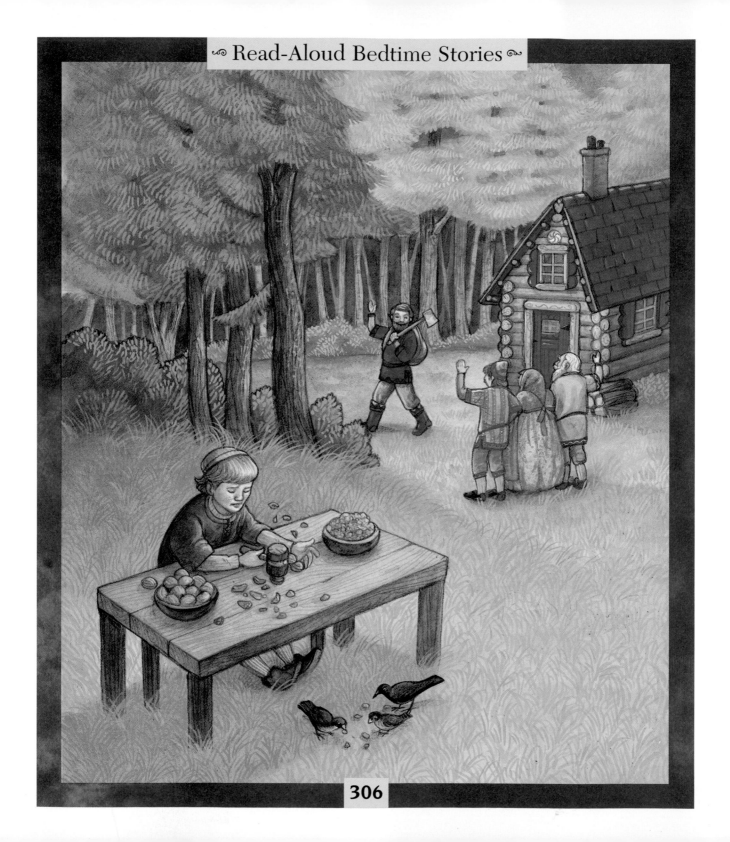

A little log cabin stood in the middle of a forest. It was home to a young boy named Samuel. He lived with his mother, father, and two older brothers.

Samuel was a kind and gentle boy. He tried very hard not to make trouble. He stayed out of the way of the others. He did what he was told. He tried to do everything well. He tried as hard as he could. But his family always found fault with him.

"You forgot to sweep under the beds," his mother always said.

"You water the plants too much," his father always said.

"You chew like a cow," his brother Tom always said.

"You hog all the covers," his brother Jack always said.

Samuel never said anything back. He just put his head down. He kept his mouth shut. He did not like to make things worse.

One day, he sat shelling nuts. They always left him alone when he was shelling nuts.

"Who will go chop some wood?" his mother asked.

Samuel did not offer to go. He knew his mother would just laugh.

"I will go," Tom said.

"Good boy," said their mother.

She kissed Tom's cheek and gave him a basket. It was filled with sweet cakes and cold lemonade. Tom took an ax and headed into the woods.

It was not long before Tom returned home. He had the ax and the lunch basket. He did not have any wood. One of his shoulders was bleeding.

"What happened, Tom?" their mother asked.

"It wasn't my fault!" Tom said. "I met a strange man in the woods. He was old and wrinkled. He started the trouble. He asked for food. Can you believe that? He wanted to get his dirty hands on my lunch!"

"What did you tell him?" Samuel asked.

He hoped Tom had helped the man.

"I told him no, of course!" Tom said. "I said there were only enough sweet cakes for me."

Tom explained what had happened next.

"I ordered the old man to get out of my way. I began chopping wood. I lost my hold on the ax. It cut my shoulder."

"What did the old man do?" Samuel asked.

"Nothing," Tom said. "He just looked happy."

Samuel could understand that. Tom had been rude to the old man. His shoulder had only a scratch. It was not even bleeding anymore.

"I will go and chop the wood," Jack said.

"Good boy," said their mother.

She kissed Jack's cheek and gave him the basket. Plenty of sweet cakes and lemonade were left. Jack took the ax and went on his way.

It was not long before Jack returned home. He carried the lunch basket. He did not have the ax. He did not have the wood. His foot was bleeding.

"What happened, Jack?" their mother asked.

"It wasn't my fault!" Jack said. "I went to finish Tom's work. That strange old man was there. Tom was right. He is a troublemaker. He asked for a drink. He wanted to get his wormy lips on my clean jug!"

"What did you tell him?" Samuel asked.

He could guess the answer.

"I told him no, of course!" Jack said. "I said there was only enough lemonade for me."

"Did you get hurt chopping wood, too?" asked Samuel.

"Yes I did, you fool," Jack said. "Somehow, the ax broke in two pieces. The blade cut my foot. That man just sat there and looked happy."

Samuel could understand that.

"I will go chop the wood," Samuel said.

His family stared at him. They laughed at him.

"Be careful not to get chopped in half," his father said.

"Silly boy," his mother said.

She did not kiss him. She did not give him sweet cakes and lemonade. He wrapped some bread and a water jug in a cloth. He picked up a new ax and went on his way.

Samuel whistled as he walked. He was not afraid to meet the old man. He wanted to meet him. He wanted to say he was sorry for his brothers. They had not been very nice.

Samuel saw Jack's broken ax on the ground. The old man sat nearby.

"Hello," he said. "I am Samuel. I think you have already met my brothers. I am sorry they were rude."

"It is not your fault," the old man said. "Will you sit with me?"

Samuel nodded and sat down.

He could see the man was very old and wrinkled. His skin made Samuel think of walnut shells. He seemed nice. His hands were not dirty. His lips were not wormy either.

"I am very thirsty and hungry," the man said. "Will you share your lunch with me?"

"Oh, yes," Samuel said. "I wish I had something good to share. I have only dry bread and warm water."

Samuel untied his cloth. It was filled with sweet cakes and a jug of lemonade. He could not believe it! He knew he had packed bread and water.

"What luck!" he said. "We will eat well!"

Samuel and the old man ate all the sweet cakes. They drank all the lemonade. It was a good lunch.

The old man had many stories to share. He was really very nice.

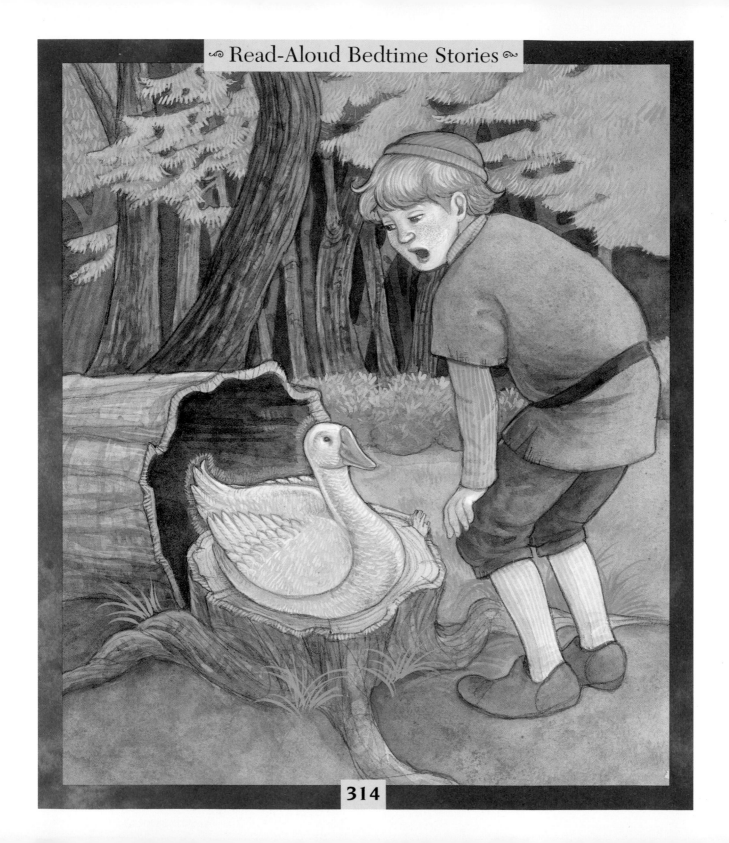

"It is time for me to go," the old man said.

Samuel did not want to say good-bye. He was having such a nice time. But he showed the man the direction of the town. He said he was sorry again for his brothers.

"I have been thinking about that," said the old man. "You are not at all like your brothers. You shared your lunch with me. You kept me company when you could have been chopping wood. You are a very kind young man."

Samuel looked down at his feet. He did not know what to say. He was not used to hearing nice words.

"I would like to repay your kindness," said the old man. "Do you see the tree with the ax marks in it?"

Samuel nodded. He saw where Tom and Jack had chopped at it.

"I kept your brothers from chopping the tree down," said the old man. "I think you should finish what they started. Look inside the tree once you cut it in two. You will find something."

The man started down the road. Samuel began to chop at the tree. His strokes were strong and sure. The tree fell with a crash. Samuel looked down into the stump.

A goose was curled up inside.

Samuel gently lifted it out. He held it in his arms. It was smooth and soft. Its feathers were golden!

The goose was special. Samuel could not take it home. How could he keep it? He was not worthy of something so special. He needed to find the old man for help.

Samuel ran to the road. There was no sign of the old man. He started toward town. He held onto the goose. He passed other travelers on the way. He noticed their stares and whispers. He looked at his feet. He tried not to listen.

"They think I'm stupid," he thought.

The people were not talking about Samuel. They were talking about the golden goose. It was quite a sight.

Three sisters saw the goose. They could not believe it. They had to touch it to see if it was real.

"Me first!" said the oldest sister.

"No, me!" said the other two at once.

The younger girls grabbed their sister to stop her. The oldest girl touched the goose at the same time. She could not pull away. She was stuck to the goose! Her sisters were stuck to her! They had no choice but to follow.

"Stop trying to steal that goose," a judge said to the girls.

He grabbed the last girl in line. He got stuck, too.

"Leave my girls alone," the mother of the girls said.

She grabbed the judge's coat. She also got stuck.

Samuel noticed none of this. He was too busy trying to ignore everyone. The line of people behind him grew and grew.

Samuel's hopes fell when he reached town. People packed the square. He would never find the old man in the crowd. He looked anyway. Wherever he went, a line of people followed behind.

The people of the town were acting strange. Some were making funny faces. Some were throwing pies at each other. Some were doing silly dances.

"Why is everyone acting so strange?" Samuel asked one man.

The man was balancing a pickle on his nose.

"For the princess," the man with the pickle said. "She cannot laugh. Not one giggle. Not one chuckle. The king just wants to make his daughter laugh. He promises half his land to whoever makes it happen."

The man pointed to a balcony above them. Samuel saw the king. He stood next to the princess. She looked very serious. Nobody could make her laugh. Samuel felt bad for her.

He decided to ask the princess why she was unhappy. He knew what it was like to be unhappy. Maybe he could help her. He called to her. She looked down from the balcony.

What she saw looked like a giant, wiggly worm. It was made of many people and one golden goose. The princess watched them tug and pull and twist. She started to laugh!

The princess laughed and laughed. She fell off of her chair.

"Who made my wish come true?" the king asked.

Samuel saw the princess point to him. He was sure she was pointing at someone else. He turned around to look. He saw everyone behind him for the first time. It made him laugh, too.

"How did you do this?" the princess asked Samuel.

"I do not know," Samuel said. "I found this special goose in the forest. A friend helped me. I am trying to find that friend."

"You say this is a special goose?" asked the king. "What makes it special? What causes such sticky problems?"

"It was a test," said a voice in the crowd.

It was the old man.

"The goose is under a magic spell," he said. "The hand that touches it in disbelief will stick to its feathers. Samuel believed such a goose could exist. He also believed in me. He did not stick to the goose. Everyone else did."

The old man touched each person stuck to the golden goose. Each one finally came free. He lifted the goose from Samuel's arms.

"Go claim the king's reward," the old man said. "I must go."

Samuel would miss him. They were friends.

"You must come and visit," Samuel said. "I will have half of the king's land. There will be plenty to share."